BOOK TWO OF THE GIFTED WORLD SERIES

THE BURNS CONFLICT

L. D. VALENCIA

Copyright © 2020 L. D. Valencia

All Rights Reserved. No part of this publication may be reproduced in any form or by any means, including scanning, photocopying, or otherwise without prior written permission of the copyright holder.

First Printing, 2020

Printed in the United States of America

Dedication

To our little Valentine and Ruby.

You will always be in our hearts.

Contents

PROLOGUE: SOME TIME AGO	1
FILE #01 TRYOUTS	5
FILE #02 DEBRIEFING	11
FILE #03 THE MENTOR	19
FILE #04 THE THREE SUSPECTS	24
FILE #05 THE FIRST MISSION	29
FILE #06 THE BASICS	37
FILE #07 THE OTHER INTERN	46
FILE #08 THE GHOST	51
FILE #09 THE UNDERGROUND	57
FILE #10 THE MEET	64
FILE #11 THE SUBSTITUTE	71
FILE #12 EYE OF THE STORM	79
FILE #13 THE CHEATER	88
FILE #14 A TALE OF TWO AGENTS	96
FILE #15 MIND GAMES	104
FILE #16 JOIN THE UNDERGROUND	114
FILE #17 THE CONCERT	117
FILE # 18 A QUESTION OF GREATNESS	126
FILE #19 FALLEN FIGURES	131
FILE #20 INTO THE UNDERGROUND	139
FILE #21 BROTHERS IN ARMS	145
FILE #22 BROTHERS IN SCARS	152
FILE #23 ANOTHER WHITE ROOM	159
EPILOGUE	166
ABOUT THE AUTHOR	169

PROLOGUE
SOME TIME AGO

An old man sat at his computer screen, typing feverishly. He turned to his side to cough into his hand. Looking at his fingers, he saw a splotchy mess of red-stained mucus. A pain ran through his chest, causing him to clutch his left side. The world began to spin. The screen blurred into a whirlwind of color.

After steadying himself against the desk with both hands, he was able to center himself. The dizziness subsided, and he could see straight again. His fits were getting more frequent, and his age was beginning to show. He finally decided to call it a night.

So, he packed up all of his things into his briefcase. His medicine, a folder that said, "Papers to Grade", and his leftover ham and cheese sandwich. As he clicked it closed, he looked around the room. For years, he had made this office his home. However, this wasn't his real job. This wasn't his real calling.

His was a life that was like many of the gifted individuals of the world. Many agents led lives that were not what they appeared. Many had to hide what they really did for national security for personal beliefs.

Running a finger over the engraving on the briefcase that read "Drake", the old man decided to leave. He locked the door behind him and went down the hallway to the elevator. Several cleaning bots hummed past him as they cleaned the floors. Inside the elevator, he coughed again. He spat on the floor and dragged his foot over it.

He wiped his mouth with a handkerchief. With a sigh, he ran his hand over his bald head. Another reminder of his age. At one point, he'd had a thick head of hair, as dark as midnight. But not anymore. Now, he was bald, old, and diseased.

"What is this life coming to?" he asked himself.

The elevator dinged, and he stepped off. He walked down the entrance hallway, nodded at the security guard, and exited the building. Outside, the cold air was bracing. It was the kind of night air that cut through your body. It stabbed like a knife.

Dr. Drake stopped at a bench, set down his briefcase, and put his beanie over his head. In a futile attempt to warm his hands, he brought them together and blew into them. It helped for all of five seconds.

Just then, a figure stepped out of the shadows. He stood beside a tree in a casual way, his right leg draped across his left leg. His right arm was leaning against the tree's trunk. "Cold night, isn't it?" the figure asked in a smooth Spanish accent.

"That seems like an understatement," Drake replied.

"It's the first night of winter," the figure replied, taking his first step toward Drake.

Instinctively, Drake took a step away. He didn't necessarily fear this man. In honesty, he made no threats or presented himself in a nefarious way. But still, something about him seemed menacing.

"Oh, don't worry," the figure said. "I am not here to hurt you. I actually am here to help you."

"Help me?" Drake replied. "How do you mean?"

"Let's take a walk."

As they strolled, the man didn't speak for several steps. It was as if he wanted to build the anticipation. Drake analyzed the situation. Based on the man's situation, Drake assessed that he was playing a game. He was attempting to show his authority in the situation so he made Drake wait on him.

Drake sized him up as they walked. He had long dark hair speckled with grey throughout, and he had it pulled back in a ponytail. His circular glasses sat on the tip of his nose, and a red scarf was wrapped around his neck. He wore a long black pea coat and fine leather shoes.

After some time, the man finally spoke up. He was obviously well-schooled as he spoke eloquently and with perfect diction. "Well, my friend, my organization would like to partner with you."

"Oh, why is that?" Drake asked.

"We heard that your funding has been pulled."

"How would you know that?"

"It is our job to know what agencies are up to these days."

"So, you're an intelligence agency?" Drake asked.

"No, not at all. We are just a group of concerned citizens. We just have the means of finding out what is happening in this world."

"So, why would you want to fund my research?"

"We believe that your research has many practical applications. Our..." He paused for a moment as if to find the word. "Our president thinks that we should be in business together."

"Well, I believe that my research has practical benefits as well. But some feel the risks outweigh its potential," Drake answered, his fist clenching tighter around his briefcase.

"As we speak, my organization is willing to make you an offer."

"Really? Without a demonstration or expense report?" The surprise was obvious in his tone.

"Dr. Drake, my group and I are not the kind that likes to spend time waiting for what we want. If you cannot deliver, we will simply cut ties and be done," the man said, running his finger across his neck as he said the word "cut".

The doctor's eyes focused on him. "And if I decide to find another option?"

"Oh, we don't think you will. Not if you want word of what really happened to Dr. Ferentheil getting out."

Drake turned to face him, his eyes wide and his mouth ajar.

"Yes, good sir. We know about that as well."

"I see," Drake answered. "Well, then."

"So, do we have a deal?" asked the man.

"Yes, I suppose so."

"Good to be in business with you, Dr. Drake. My name is Pius."

FILE #01

TRYOUTS

He was panting ferociously. A stitch in his side was swelling. He faked to the right and then moved left. Sweat poured down his forehead. Then a punch came straight at him. His fake hadn't worked.

Why am I here? he thought. *Why did I put myself in this position?*

Gabriel blocked the first punch with his left arm. For a split second, he felt like he was going to be all right. He dropped and tried to sweep her leg, but the opponent back away just in time.

The sun was shining into the room, and he knew that gave his opponent an edge. Somehow, she absorbed the sunshine like a flower. It made her faster, stronger, and deadlier.

Her barrage came in so quickly that Gabriel couldn't stop them all. She threw two punches in quick succession. He blocked the first with his right arm and protected himself from the second with a telekinetic shield. Then she struck with a kick from an off-balance position. He moved to counter. However, the kick was a feint. She came high with another punch.

The punch connected, and Gabriel dropped to the ground. A voice called out, "That's one for Katrina."

Gabriel looked at the scoreboard. It read 3-1. He jumped back up and readied himself for the next phase. A man in a black and white striped shirt said, "Go!"

Katrina, an auburn-haired girl, jumped up and came down with a fist. Her speed was inhuman. Jake had told him that her gift was solar absorption, and he was getting to see how it worked first-hand. Even though he was starting to understand the impressive nature of her power, he didn't have any kind of an edge.

Although, he had managed to earn a point early, as the fight continued on, it seemed to favor her more and more. Her speed, strength, and agility all seemed to be improving as the fight went on. As Gabriel was getting slower and more tired, she seemed to be getting faster and stronger.

He managed to block her attack, and in the moment before she landed, he spotted a small opening. He pushed out with his mind, and she lost her balance. Then he threw his shoulder into her and knocked her to the ground.

The voice from before, rough and gravely, called out. "Three to two, with Katrina in the lead."

Katrina stood back up and rubbed her shoulder. She had landed on her left side with a tremendous crash. Gabriel hoped that she didn't have quickened healing from the sunlight as well. Otherwise, that hit might not even matter.

Quickly, both combatants returned to their starting spots. She had both of her hands clenched in fists, showing an aggressive stance, while Gabriel had adopted a sideways stance with his hands out, open-palmed.

Gabriel knew that his gift was a more defensive one. Simon had told him that he was a "Tank," which was a video game term. It was the character in a game that was mostly defensive and able to take a lot of hits. Here it meant that Gabriel's telekinesis was able to defend against almost any attack, and he needed to use it to his advantage.

Just like before, Katrina jumped in to make an attack. She moved quicker than he expected and delivered a punch-kick combo that forced Gabriel to backpedal. He was off-balance and left himself wide open. She lunged forward but stayed low. Then she threw a hand forward that emitted a beam of light that felt like a punch to his gut. Immediately, Gabriel dropped to the ground on his back.

"That will be enough," the raspy voice called out. It was Coach V, watching from the sideline.

The dimmed overhead lights were turned back on to full brightness. Standing to his feet, Gabriel could see the scene around him. Several uniformed students were all around the ring watching. A few sweaty students were watching interestedly, but some with towels around their necks started whispering to each other. Gabriel was the last to compete so everyone was relaxed now.

Coach V had been scribbling notes on his tablet the whole fight. Gabriel had seen him doing so during the other fights. As each match drew on, he would watch and note what he liked or disliked. The ever-informant Simon told him that Coach V somehow knew just from watching the sparring which fighters had it and which ones didn't. Gabriel wondered what pathetic remarks he had made about his performance. He knew there was mostly criticism to be made.

The team gathered around the coach as he started making announcements. It was the third day of tryouts for the sparring team. The first day was a rigorous day of workouts and exercises, as well as running; a lot of running. Gabriel hated running. It was one thing if it was part of a sport, like in a soccer game. But running just for the sake of running drove him crazy. In a sport, you get that adrenaline rush when chasing an opponent or going after the ball. But just sprinting with no goal seemed like the most boring thing ever.

The extensive workout from the first day knocked out about half of the hopefuls. Then the second day was more of a training routine. Coach asked each of the remaining individuals to show off their Gifts in order to determine how adept they were. This knocked out those that had poor control over their gifts. Then today was the combat training.

Because the sparring team was the hand-to-hand combat team, the fighters could use their gifts in the ring. The basic premise was to earn points by knocking your opponent down with either physical attacks or your gifts. Jake had been on the team last year, but he didn't compete at all. Mostly because he was a freshman, but also because he didn't have great control. So, Coach V had sat him.

Just as Gabriel and Katrina got out of the ring, Coach was explaining his method of evaluation. Then he and Simon went around handing each potential candidate a printed-out piece of paper with his notes. "At the bottom, you will see whether you need to come back tomorrow."

When Coach V got to Gabriel, he paused and thumbed through his papers. Coach found Gabriel's and handed it to him. "Here you are, Gabe."

Gabriel chewed on his lip in anticipation. He tried to give a smile, but it was a half-hearted one at best. He said his thanks as Coach V continued on.

He skimmed through the top portion, which was covered in notes. He saw words like, "Good defensive stance," "poor attack method," and "needs to be more decisive." Then he found the bottom. He had made it. A wave of relief washed over him. His tense shoulders dropped as he exhaled, possibly for the first time all day.

Jake rushed over to Gabriel with a look of anticipation on his face. "So, how'd you do?" he asked, almost cringing.

"I made it!"

"Oh nice! That's great. I was worried for a minute," Jake answered. "You didn't look excited so I was worried."

"I'm more relieved than anything."

Coach V called everyone to attention. "Congratulations to those of you who made it, and I am sorry to those of you that didn't. Please try out next year. Keep working at it, and honing your gift. I have faith in you."

Gabriel listened intently as Coach V explained. Only Coach V could tell people they didn't make it and still let them leave feeling like there was still hope. Gabriel admired that about Coach.

As the contestants trickled out of the gymnasium's arena, Coach V waved his hand to summon Gabriel. He immediately threw his bag over his shoulder and rushed over to Coach.

"Can you meet me in my office in five minutes?"

"Sure," Gabriel answered with a tinge of worry.

"All right, thank you." Then Coach walked out of the arena and down the hall where the offices were located.

Gabriel told Eames and Jake that he needed to meet with Coach, and that he would catch them later for dinner. Although his stomach was growling with hunger, Gabriel was curious about what Coach V wanted.

When he made it down the hall toward Coach V's office, he noticed how quiet it was. After a few turns through lonely hallways, Gabriel made it to Coach V's office. He knocked on the thick wooden door. Through the glass, Gabriel could see Coach V waving him in.

He was taking a phone call and mimed an apology, but he pointed for Gabriel to take a seat.

"Well, sir," Coach said on the phone, "I have my next appointment here. Can I speak with you later about the details?"

He paused for a reply.

"All right, thank you. Have a good day, sir."

"Was that Dean Einrich?" Gabriel asked.

Coach V paused, as if he didn't understand the question. There was a slight stutter, then he answered, "Yes, actually, it was."

"He seems like a cool guy. I had him for my first course last year."

"Yes, he is a very cool guy," Coach V answered with a laugh. "I respect him a lot for the work he does."

Gabriel nodded in reply.

Then Coach V sat up and took a more serious posture. "Gabriel, the reason I wanted to talk to you today was because I need to tell you something."

"All right." Gabriel was sure it was about his very poor performance in the ring. "I think I know what it's about."

"Mmm, I doubt that."

Gabriel squinted in confusion. "Uh," was all he could muster.

"We need to discuss your visitor this summer," Coach V stated.

"What do you mean? When my grandmother visited? She visits all the time. Why do you want to know about my grandma?" Gabriel asked, his tone getting higher pitched with each word.

"No, no, no," Coach said, motioning like a crossing guard forcing a car to stop. "I need to know about the agent you met this summer."

"How...how do you know about that?"

"Well..." Coach V started, but then Gabriel sprang up.

"Who told you about that?" Gabriel's voice cracked and quaked.

"Gabriel, please calm down. I am part of the Organization."

FILE #02

DEBRIEFING

Instantly, Gabriel was transported back to that day. He remembered it like it was yesterday.

***

It was the first day of June. Gabriel received an email from Captain Duo. Duo was one who brought in the agents that rescued Gabriel and his friends from Dr. Drake. Just as their fight with Drake was turning deadly, Duo and his agents came in to save them. Gabriel was then told that Duo worked for an "Organization", as he put it. However, he never told Gabriel what it was called.

In the email, Gabriel was asked to come the library in Bethlehem. He got there at 11am like the email designated. He stood at the entrance and waited. But then he realized that for some reason, no one was there. Children and parents walked in and out of the building, but he didn't see anyone that looked like they were an agent. So, he decided to walk inside.

Inside, he walked past the main desk, stopped for a moment, and thought about asking them if they'd seen any special agents recently. But he decided that was a bad idea. *I sure don't understand how this whole agency thing works,* he thought to himself.

He walked down the first aisle of books. A girl, not much older than himself, walked into him and looped her arm through his. She pulled him as if they were a couple walking along the shelves of books.

As she pulled him, she whispered, "Act cool. Okay."

She pulled him to a corner of the library and walked around a beam. In front of them was a mask of shadow. Gabriel noticed her eyes shimmer with a darkness, and the shadow opened into a doorway.

"Let's go," she said in a nonchalant tone. Without waiting for a reply, she walked through the shadow and into a room.

Gabriel's eyes widened. He held his hand to his forehead and smiled. "That was amazing..."

"Let's go, Green," the girl's voice called from inside the shadow.

With a start, he jumped through the portal and into a dark room. Inside, he saw three people sitting at a table. Even though all of the lights were on, the area around them was cast in a dark shadow. It was as if the area was being purposefully masked.

On the left, he could make out what appeared to be a girl with shoulder-length hair. She didn't look much older than Gabriel. He noticed her eyes glowed with a strange darkness. It was the girl from before. She must be able to manipulate shadows. At the head of the table was a lithe man with short, red hair. The last was a thicker man, who sat to the right of the man in the center.

"Are you the person I'm supposed to be meeting?" asked Gabriel. Through the shadow, Gabriel could just barely see the person nod.

Gabriel's instructions said that he was supposed to confirm the identity of his contact by using a specific pass phrase. So, he cleared his throat and then said, "A star shines in Bethlehem."

The man nodded and said in a thick accent, "And the three magi have arrived."

Gabriel tried to place the accent. It was Irish from his best guess. The man stood up and Gabriel could see him better now. It was a thin man, with very red hair. He had glasses and wore a suit, just like the other agents he saw. However, the noticed that his man wasn't wearing a suit jacket, but instead he wore a dark gray vest with the same color slacks.

The man motioned for Gabriel to have a seat at the table across from him. So, tentatively, he walked over to the table and did just that.

"Well then," the man said in his thick accent. "Shall we begin?"

"Sure," Gabriel answered.

"Very well, my name is Agent Insomnia."

"I'm Gabr..."

"Please, sir, I know exactly who you are," Insomnia replied, combining the words 'you' and 'are'. "Gabriel Green. Born in Bethlehem, Pennsylvania. Current Student at SIA. Year: Sophomore. Department: Kinetics. Gift: Telekinesis."

Gabriel's jaw dropped unintentionally and he closed it as nonchalantly as possible. He nodded very forcefully. *Stop nodding so much.*

"Gabriel, I have been watching you for some time now. I am an intelligence specialist for the, uh...Organization and like m' name implies, I don't sleep. So, I watch everything. Ever since you got on the Organization's radar, I have been keeping tabs on you."

"What? Why?" asks Gabriel, somewhat concerned.

"Well, for your safety mostly. We've had agents on call, in case you-know-who made a play at coming for you. Also, you are being designated as a VIP, a very important person."

Gabriel did know who. Last semester, Dr. Drake had kidnapped Serena and himself. He had nefarious plans for them, and he used Serena for her gift. He had tested on others too. Students who he either took blood from or experimented on. But Drake wasn't the old man anymore. He was now a younger version of himself. Somehow, he had gotten himself a new body, and he had Serena use her telepathy to transfer his mind into the new body. Luckily, the Organization stepped in and helped them when things got really bad. Unfortunately, Drake had gotten away.

Gabriel placed both hands on the table and asked, "Why are you telling me all of this?"

"As a VIP, we are giving you more intel than the usual person. We want to keep you safe, m' lad. We have your best interests at heart."

"Oh, uh, thank you," Gabe replied, stuttering.

"Now, to the task at hand," the agent said. "You have accepted an intern-based position in our Organization."

"Well, Duo asked me if I was interested in becoming an agent. I always loved how agents help save people and do heroic things to protect the world."

"Well, yes, that is true. We aren't cape crusaders like the comic books, but we do our best to help."

Agent Insomnia then gave Gabriel a basic breakdown of what the role of an agent was. "Essentially, the agencies exist to help keep order. As I am sure you know, when the Transit of Venus first gave people powers, the world was a wee bit rumbly."

Gabriel held a hand up to pause him. "A what now?"

"Rumbly, like dodgy or crazy," Insomnia explained. "Forgive me, I am from Ireland so my phrases sometimes aren't understood by others."

"No problem. Uh, go on, please."

Insomnia continued. "Anyway, when the world first experienced these powers, some parts of the world were hurt. Other parts still haven't recovered. So, the United Nations created the agencies to help take back order and keep it."

"And you work for one of these agencies, right?"

"Yes, we are one of these agencies."

Gabriel nodded. "Are these two with you also agents?"

Insomnia nodded then continued, "As an agent, your duties are to take assignments from the higher ups. Complete the mission, while keeping your role discrete and in some cases unknown to those around you."

"What kind of missions?" asked Gabriel.

"We take on requests on everything from reconnaissance to hostage negotiation, from body guarding to even terrorist nullification." He paused for a moment. "We are peacekeeping task forces, us agencies. So, we do whatever we can to protect that peace."

"That sounds awesome. How can I help?"

"Well, I don't know how much Captain Duo told you, but essentially you are a trainee. We have an intern program. You will receive a mentor who will work with you to help you progress."

"Well I go to college. So, can he meet me on campus?" Gabriel asked.

Agent Insomnia smirked. "Yes, we have someone on campus that will do just fine."

"Oh, cool. Is it Simon Cruz? I know him already."

"No, but he will be staying on campus for the time being. We have more work for him to do."

"Then who?" asked Gabriel.

"I cannot tell you just yet, because he is undercover at the moment."

"How will I know when I see him?"

Agent Insomnia then said, "You know the passphrase we gave you to meet us?"

Gabriel nodded in answer.

"We will give you a new one. When he or she presents themselves to you on campus, you will say this to them. Then they will give you the proper response."

"What is the passphrase?"

"We will send it to you when you meet him," the agent answered.

"Okay, then. What now?"

"Well, we need to get your statement on the events around what we are calling the One-Thirds Betrayal."

"The what?"

"Oh, right. Well during the event you became involved in with Drake, he somehow convinced about one-third of our agents to turncoat. These agents betrayed the Organization and turned on them."

"So, that's why they were fighting and attacking each other. I thought maybe Drake had some sort of mind control gift."

"That remains to be seen, however, it didn't appear in our screenings."

With an exhale, Gabriel said, "Alright, so you just want me to tell you everything that happened?"

"Yes, please. From the beginning."

So, Gabriel told him everything that happened during his time that year. He told the agents about how he heard some rumors about the kids not remembering whole days at a time. Then about how Serena went missing. He gave him all of the details about his own kidnapping, about Jake and Simon's help. Then about the fight with Drake.

Just then, a thought came to Gabriel. "Will you guys be going to see Jake Burns, too? He's my friend."

Insomnia paused for a moment and thought. "Yes, most likely. As an individual involved in this incident, we will be needing to get his statement for our files. We will also be needing him to sign a few forms."

"What forms?" Gabriel asked with a confused expression on his face.

"These forms," the agent said, passing an open folder toward Gabe. "These all say that you are working in compliance with our Organization and that we are protecting you. In exchange for our protection, you will not share anything about the Organization's presence on campus or our dealings with Dr. Drake. Failing to do so will see you expelled from our agency, and you will be hit with a cease-and-desist order from the Protectorate for leaking matters of international security."

Gabriel was shocked for a moment. The agent made a motion with his hand lifting his jaw. Gabriel hadn't even realized it, but his mouth was hanging open again. Immediately, he snapped it shut with a clack of his teeth.

The agent then looked into Gabriel's eyes. He stared intently at him. His face became even more serious than before. "This is standard procedure, Mr. Green. Even though agencies are not 'secret organizations', much of our work is very sensitive. If someone leaked our agents, locations, or other information, lives would be at stake. Do you understand that?"

"Oh, I am...Sorry. I didn't really think of it that way."

"Well I hope you now understand how serious it is."

Agent Insomnia pointed to the folder in front of him. "Are you still interested in joining?"

Gabriel weighed his options. Although he was afraid of the responsibility, he knew that he had a chance to do something great. To help make the world a better place. He grabbed the pen on top of the papers and began signing his name to the bottom of the forms.

"Done," Gabriel said as he finished and slammed the pen down for emphasis.

Agent Insomnia began looking over the documents and then placed the folder back into his brown leather satchel. He stood up, brushed his hair back, and then held out a hand. Gabriel stood up as well and shook Insomnia's hand.

"So, you guys are pretty serious about not spilling the beans?" he asked in a joking tone.

"Yes, most dearly. If you do, you will be detained until we can make sure no other lives are at stake. After that, we can't protect you, nor will we. Not to mention whatever legal situations come from the Protectorate."

Gabriel's eyes widened. He wasn't sure, but he thought that might be a threat.

Agent Insomnia threw his satchel strap over his shoulder and crossed it over his chest. He motioned to the two agents beside him. They stood up as well. The man to his side turned and disappeared through the shadows behind them.

"You know, Gabriel, some of us see your potential. I hope you're worth all the trouble we're going to in order to train you," said Insomnia.

The young man's eyes lifted up to meet the agent's. Although his words were heavy, he looked at Gabriel with a hopeful expression. Then the agent walked away backwards, never turning away from him.

"We will be watching, Gabriel. And we will be in contact with you."

"To make sure that I don't mess up?" he asked.

"No," Insomnia replied. He paused. "Well, yes, but also to keep you safe."

Insomnia saluted Gabriel as he backed up toward the shadows. In an instant, he had disappeared. Gabriel looked over to the girl with the short, dark hair. She brushed the hair out of her face, and he noticed a row of earrings along one ear. She motioned for him to turn around.

As he did, the portal opened up to the library. He walked through, and as he did, he turned to thank her. But the portal was gone. "Cheery bunch," he said under his breath.

FILE #03

THE MENTOR

Gabriel shook his head as he snapped back to reality. He looked back at Coach. Was he really the contact that Agent Insomnia told him about? For a second, he didn't know how to respond. Then he remembered what Insomnia said.

"Success is not a good teacher," Gabriel said, remembering the quote that Agent Insomnia had sent him through an encrypted message.

Coach V tipped his hat up and he looked directly into Gabriel's eyes. "But failure makes you humble."

Gabriel's expression softened. He sighed in relief. "Phew."

As he slumped back in the chair, Coach V pulled a small device from his desk. He placed the small black device, no bigger than a wristwatch, in between Gabriel and himself. It looked like a black, plastic rectangle with curved edges. Gabriel's brow furrowed as he looked at it. Coach V pushed a button on it and returned to his seat.

"What is that?" Gabriel asked.

Coach V glanced around the room. "Just for security purposes. After Drake's betrayal last year, we're all a little more on edge. We've had the room swept for bugs, but we can't be too cautious. There are plenty of gifts that we can't trace."

"That's awesome," Gabriel said, intrigued.

"Gabriel, the reason why I wanted to meet with you was to let you know that I will be your mentor, and you will be my intern."

"That's right," Gabriel said, realizing that this was the moment that Insomnia told him about.

"Have you been briefed on the general expectations of an agent?"

Gabriel nodded. "Yeah, I met Agent Insomnia over the summer. He told me a little about what you agents do."

"All right, so what is it you think an agent's job is?" Coach V asked propping his elbows up on the desk and tenting his fingers in front of him.

"Well, uh, they..." Gabriel's voice trailed off as he thought of an answer.

Coach V sat for a moment, waiting for Gabriel's reply. When nothing came, Coach said, "I won't bore you with the details of how the agencies started, but when the agencies were founded, they were given the task of maintaining order to keep the world safe. There are bad people out there, and it is our job to help make the world a little safer."

"So, you guys are the good guys, kind of like superheroes?" Gabriel asked, uncertain.

"Somewhat. Generally, our organization takes on difficult mission requests that require immediate attention. Sometimes these are from governments, and other times, they're from companies. We've even taken mission requests from individuals on rare occasion."

Excitedly, Gabriel asked, "Were you guys involved in the rescue of that European Prime Minister this summer?"

Coach V dropped his hands into his lap. He didn't answer for a long time and ran a hand through his graying stubble. "This relationship—the mentor, disciple relationship, that is—

it is a very special one. So, I think I'll tell you. Yes, we did help in that mission."

"That's awesome," Gabriel said with more excitement than intended.

Coach V coughed into his hand. "Uh, yes, it was a rather beneficial mission. Any time the mission goes well, it is a good day."

"Do they not go well often?"

"Not exactly, but it is a dangerous occupation. And, yes, there is a certain celebrity that comes with being an agent. People like Endeavor and Render have become household names. But missions are dangerous. There are many times that an agent doesn't come home."

Gabriel's face fell. He looked at the ground, as if studying the blue carpet. However, he was weighing the cost of risking his own life vs helping the world. Would he be willing to risk his life in order to save someone else?

Before he could answer the question, Coach changed the topic. "Anyway, as your mentor, I will be overseeing your training. Fortunately, my cover here on campus will help with that."

"True."

"Gabriel, your telekinesis is a very unique and powerful gift. I want you to focus on the defensive capabilities that come with it."

"You mean my shielding?"

"Exactly. It has massive potential to protect and save," Coach V answered, placing his hand on the dark oak desk.

Gabriel nodded in agreement. Just last semester, he'd used his telekinetic ability to shield himself and his friends against Drake's onslaught. Coach V could see it in Gabriel's eyes. He was thinking about that day.

How could he not? Coach V wondered. That had been a horrifying experience. "How are you doing after the incident with Drake?"

"Uh, I think I am okay," Gabriel answered in a shaky tone, still not looking up at Coach.

Coach V was not convinced. His gift gave extra him more insight and intuition into situations than a normal person. He squirmed in his seat for a moment, trying to find the words. "What's bothering you about it?" he asked.

Gabriel's head snapped up and he looked into Coach's eyes. They were a similar color to Gabriel's, but his were a darker stone gray. "It was a terrifying experience honestly. I've had nightmares since then. Not every night, but once in a while. Agent Insomnia told me that I had agents looking out for me so that's helped, but it still worries me."

"Gabriel, we live in a dangerous world. And I wish it was made safer by the gifts we received, but in all honesty, it's probably more dangerous now. Yes, in many ways, the world is better off. We have clean energy, thanks to the gifted. We aren't at risk of nuclear war anymore. But in a lot of ways, it's more unpredictable than ever before."

Gabriel's expression fell again.

Coach V stood and walked around his desk. He leaned against the edge and placed a hand on Gabriel's shoulder. "But that doesn't mean we can allow our fear to cripple us. We have the power to change the world. right?"

Gabriel looked up and nodded. "You're right." Then a thought came into Gabriel's head. He never found out what ever happened to Drake. "Can you tell me what happened to Drake?" asked Gabriel.

"Well, for the most part, we don't know. However, we do believe that he defected to an unknown group. He had it too well planned, too well orchestrated, for him to have been working alone. Someone or something was giving him the funding for his experiments, and it wasn't the college or the Guild."

"Do you know where he could have gone?" Gabriel asked.

"We have some leads on his whereabouts, but nothing very substantial. The captains have decided to split the teams up into two groups. One group will continue to look for him, but the other group is going to start searching his lab."

"That's a good idea. Maybe you can find some clues there."

"Hopefully. Simon has been combing through all the data on his servers, but he hasn't found much. Because of Drake's mental gift, he didn't store much data on his servers. So, the information we've found has been slim at best."

Gabriel thought for a moment. "What group would want to help Drake?"

Coach V raised his hand to scratch the back of his head. He was looking at something on a far shelf, but Gabriel couldn't tell what. "We don't really know who is helping him. We have a few theories on who it *could* be, but that's all, really."

"So," Gabriel said. "Let me see if I understand this. Dr. Drake used to work for the Organization. But he betrayed your group and now is working with some shadow group?"

"Basically, that's what all our evidence is pointing to."

"Man, I feel like I am living in a comic book," said Gabriel, leaning back in his chair.

"Except in the comic books, the bad guys want some unattainable goal, like ruling the world. These people we're dealing with now, we don't know who they are. Usually, the villains in comic books are well-known. Plus, they wear costumes so you know who they are. Real villains could be the people you think you can trust. They could be anyone. They could be on this very campus."

FILE #04

THE THREE SUSPECTS

Gabriel's eyes widened. "What do you mean? Are they really on campus?"

"Like I said, our specialist, Simon, has been combing through the data that Dr. Drake was collecting. Most of it was kept off the record. Because of his gift, he doesn't need to record his findings. He just remembers everything."

Gabriel nodded. Drake had gone on at length about his mental abilities. His Gift gave him the ability to mentally process and think at super speeds. It would make sense that he could practically never forget anything.

"However, it seemed he was communicating with someone on campus using a secure network. Simon found it, even though it was being routed through several channels. Gosh, we sure are lucky that kid is so skilled," Coach said with a smirk.

Gabriel smiled in return. "He sure is. He saved us down there that day. If he hadn't been able to send a message, we would never had survived."

"That's for sure. When I received his message, I got an idea how gifted he really was."

"Wait, you got the message?" Gabriel asked. "You were working on that mission?"

"Of course. Who do you think was his superior?"

Gabriel hadn't really thought about it, but it made sense.

"Anyway," Coach continued. "We believe that he could be Drake's contact and is posing as a professor."

Coach V put his hand on his chin and rubbed it through the hefty amount of graying stubble. Meanwhile, Gabriel did the same thing through the almost unnoticeable amount of peach fuzz on his own chin.

"What I am going to propose to you might be dangerous, but it might help us figure out where this person is,"

"What is it?" Gabriel asked.

"I want you to get into the classes of a few of our suspects," Coach answered.

"Sounds good. Who are your suspects?"

Coach V turned on the large screen behind his desk and pointed to the board. Three pictures showed up on the screen. Each was a campus professor's ID picture. They all had the same fake smile, as if they were being forced to do so. "These are our three suspects,"

"What makes you think it's one of these three?" asked Gabriel.

"For starters, these three all are newer hires. They've all only worked at the school for a few months, whereas the other professors have been working here for much longer. Secondly, we have already worked on clearing the other professors and staff members alibis and backgrounds. These three all haven't been cleared yet."

"Okay, I guess that makes sense."

"Plus," Coach V added, "each of them gives me a strange feeling. I think it's my gift telling me that they aren't to be trusted."

"All right," Gabriel answered. "So, tell me about them."

He pointed to the first on the left. "Professor Eleanor Ross. Works in the Transmutation Department in the Gifted Program. She has no previous record. However, she did have affiliation with some extreme Gifted Groups in her youth. So, she may still be tied to these groups."

Gabriel took out a notebook and was about to write that down, when Coach V yelled for him to stop. "Don't do that, Gabriel!"

"Why not?" he asked.

"The campus is not a secure location. We've already had people kidnapped, remember? What makes you think that if someone knows you're working with us, that they won't search your room?"

"I guess I didn't think of that."

"It's okay," Coach said. "You've been working for us for all of fifteen minutes. I don't expect you to know the do's and don'ts yet."

Gabriel smirked half-heartedly. This was so different. Now he had to think about each and every action he took. Every conversation he had. Everything could expose his work. Add that to the million other things he had to work on this semester.

"Since you don't need to take her course, I'll look into her story and see if she's our contact or not on my own. You will focus on these next two suspects."

Gabriel nodded.

"So, the next suspect is Professor Timothy Shepherd. Author of the book, *The Venusian Sky*. He is a science professor who thinks that several historical figures were gifted as well."

"Hey, I'm taking his class this semester already," said Gabriel.

"Oh, I know," answered Coach V without any explanation. "I had your advisor recommend that course because of this mission."

Gabriel made a sort of *well, that's fortunate* face.

"Now, part of me thinks that this isn't our guy. He is a public figure; however, he is a very recent hire. His past is a little sorted."

"How so?" asked Gabriel.

"He has a few crimes on his record. However, they were all minor and all involved his books. Apparently, he had a bad habit of trespassing to do research for his books. He was always able to settle the conflict out of court. But just in case, we want to keep an eye on him."

"So, what exactly am I keeping an eye out for?" Gabriel asked.

"Being in their class should give you chances to ask them questions, request meetings, and other ways of gaining intelligence on them. If they are our suspect, hopefully you can find out. Your job isn't to do anything but give us eyes on them until we can figure out who the contact is."

There was a slight pause while Gabriel soaked in the information.

After a few moments of silence, Coach finally said, "Now for our final suspect. Professor Alexander Pius, professor of The Ethical Use of Gifts."

Gabriel looked at his picture. He was a man no older than forty, with long salt and pepper hair. He wore round glasses and had a devilish grin. Of all of them, he was the only one that looked comfortable in front of the camera.

"He certainly looks confident," answered Gabriel.

"Exactly, he seems like he is a chameleon. We have spotty records on him at best. He doesn't show up on any records until college. Somehow, he got into one of the best colleges in England, even though his scores were pretty poor. Then he disappeared after college. He showed back up three years ago, working as a consultant for Pharis International. Now, he is here."

"So, you think he is our guy?"

"Our records aren't intact enough to say for sure, but my instinct, my gift, is telling me that he's our guy. One odd thing

I've noticed is that every class he has taught since his first semester has been full."

"So, he's popular?"

"Beyond popular. His class is a philosophy elective so it isn't even a required course. "

Gabriel didn't seem convinced yet. "Here," he said. "Look at this." He showed Gabriel a piece of paper. It had the number of students who've attended the class for the past six semesters. "This class has been only about half-full for the last four semesters. Then a year ago, he takes it over and the class is full."

"Is that a bad thing?" Gabriel asked.

"No, not on the surface. However, I have a bad feeling about this professor. Something isn't right about him. Honestly, I hope I'm wrong, but if I'm right. I have to make sure we catch him."

As he sat there, Gabriel made a humming sound as he thought. He didn't understand how Coach's gift worked, and it was hard to trust someone based on little to no evidence. All in all, though, he had faith in Coach. "All right then."

Then Coach V went about telling Gabriel the basics of the mission. He gave him specifics on how to glean information from his suspects and a list of some very important things to do and not to do so he would be prepared to keep an eye on the professors.

FILE #05

The First Mission

The next week was the first week of classes. Coach V helped get Gabriel into each of the classes he needed to keep an eye on the three suspected professors. Coach wanted him to keep an especially close eye on Professor Pius.

Gabriel headed into class on his first day with a nervous feeling. He had the normal first day jitters, but on top of that, he felt the anticipation of the mission. He felt like a real agent, and this was his first mission. Well, if you didn't count the whole Drake incident. As he walked to class, he thought about that day. *Did that count as his first mission?*

When he entered the room, it was a large white-walled room. There was a large board at the front with several screens facing the back. There were fifteen or twenty laboratory workstations with students standing around them. Most of the workstations were full, so Gabriel moved toward the back and found an empty one. Serena and Jake walked into the room shortly after. Gabriel waved them over.

Then the professor of the class came in from the back of the room. He was an older man with a thick mustache and a potbelly. His suit jacket was made of tweed and his pants were a different shade of tan than the jacket. Once he put his things down, he headed to the board and activated the screen. A picture of a book popped up to the screen with the professor's name on it. *The Venusian Sky* by Timothy Shepherd was written across the front cover.

He turned to address the class.

"Class, my name is Professor Shepherd," he said in a gruff voice. "I have over thirty years of on-site research experience and forty years of teaching. Also, I am the author of *The Venusian Sky*, a book that begs the question: Were there any gifted individuals before the Transit of Venus that transformed thousands of people into gifted?" The professor paused and looked as if he just remembered something for a moment. He looked over to the side of the room. "Oh yes, and this is my teacher's assistant."

He pointed as a young man stood up and walked over to him. He was quite short with dark, curly hair. Gabriel's eyes bulged when he realized it was Simon. He hadn't seen Simon before because of his placement in the room.

"Is he here for the same reason I am?" he asked under his breath.

Serena looked over at him. "What?"

"Oh nothing," Gabriel replied. "Just thinking out loud."

Professor Shepherd continued talking. "This class is laboratory-based. We will be working with some interesting chemicals and in some unique situations. Safety first, so put your goggles on if you are working with any chemicals."

The professor scanned the room for any questions. No hands rose so he looked back to the board and wrote on a tablet in his hands with a digital pen. The words popped up on the screen. He wrote *Ancient Gifted* in an elaborate flurry.

Shepherd returned his gaze to the class. "Today we will be discussing the possibility of the most ancient of civilizations having gifted individuals, the Greeks."

The class readied themselves. The sounds of clicking pens could be heard as students prepare to take notes. The air filled with the sound of clacking keyboards as students began typing on their laptops. Gabriel used a tablet with a note-taking feature that transformed the user's handwriting into typed text. It was one of his favorite apps, and he could print the notes if he needed to. Although typing was the faster alternative, he preferred this method because it helped him remember the information better.

Then the lecture began. "Millennia ago, the ancient world was full of mythologies that were full of powerful beings that could do wondrous things. It is my theory that these beings, such as Hercules and Thor, were actually gifted individuals. Because of their power, they were believed to be gods."

Gabriel noticed the look of intrigue of many students around him. Likewise, Gabriel thought this was an interesting idea, but he wondered how possible it actually was. As much as he was interested by the topic at hand, Gabriel wondered how long he was going to talk about the ideas in his book. *Is this a science class or a book club?*

Professor Shepherd asked, "Now before we continue down this discussion, whom among you can tell me about the origin of our abilities?"

Several hands rose into the air. The professor called on a student in the front row. "It's from Venus, right?"

The professor made a *tsk*, *tsk*, *tsk* sound. "Well, not exactly. That's actually something of a misconception."

Another girl raised her hand. "The sun gives off powerful gamma rays, and when they pass through the planet Venus, they're altered in a way that they emit enhanced gamma rays. When absorbed by a human, the human may develop into super powers."

Shepherd nodded his head. "Yes, we have found that the gamma rays, when they pass through the planet Venus, are altered. We call then Venusian Rays. It is also said that stones from Venus can be infused with these rays. I read an article that they are very rare and sold on the black market."

Then a student raised his hand. "So you're saying that the Transit was not the first time that human developed gifts? You think there have been gifted people for thousands of years?"

Shepherd looked at the young man with a mixture of wonder and confusion. Although he was asking a question that he believed he had already answered, he was also not following the prescribed procedure. "First off, young man, I asked for students to raise their hands before asking questions. To answer your question. I believe I made my point clear earlier. I do believe that it is possible, if not even likely, that there have been gifted for much longer than we believed. However, it is difficult to prove because many of the figures of legend don't have graves or tombs so we can't conduct tests to prove whether my hypothesis is correct or not."

After that, there was an air of caution in the class, and not a single student talked out of turn again. Mostly, the class continued in complete silence, aside from Shepherd's lecturing. At the end of class, students packed up to leave.

Amid the noise, Jake leaned over to Serena. In a sarcastic tone, he asked, "Was I in the right class?"

"I know. I thought this was a lab. Not part of his book press tour or something." Serena looked at Gabriel. He smiled, but he wasn't himself. "Are you all right?" she asked.

"Oh, yeah. I'm good. That was weird, wasn't it?"

Gabriel packed up and left for his second class, Ethics. According to Coach, this was the most likely target. As he exited the room, he pulled out his phone and opened his course list. He found the room number and walked in the direction of the class.

When he got there, he saw a massive crowd outside the room. He was confused. *Is this a blockbuster movie or a lecture hall?* Then he remembered what Coach V said. This class had been full every semester ever since this professor took over the class.

As Gabriel made his way into the room, he found a seat in the back. It was a packed house. There wasn't a single empty seat to be found in the large lecture room. Down on the lower floor, in the center of a huge crowd, sat a very well-dressed man. He wore a pale blue suit and glasses that covered his pale baby blue eyes. A dark brown overcoat was draped over the desk chair.

Gabriel had seen his eyes in the picture, but the photo didn't really capture how shockingly blue and captivating they were. His long dark hair, which was pulled into a crisp bun, had streaks of white through it, just like in the picture. Honestly, it made him seem more distinguished.

Several students got up to speak with him. Never had he seen this type of behavior before and it interested him. Some students were even asking for his autograph. *Am I missing something here?* Gabriel wondered.

The professor waved them away in a gesture that said that was all the signatures for which he had time. Then he stood up and looked out into the sea of faces. He started to walk up the stairs that separated the rows of desks. He was looking from the left to the right, as if able to make eye contact with every student the entire time.

"Ethics? What are ethics?" His voice was smooth, and he had a Spanish accent, but it also spoke of a traveled worldliness that gave off an air of wisdom and understanding.

Despite his question, no one answered. Gabriel could see that several students beside him sat enraptured by his words.

He spoke up again, "Ethics is defined as moral principles that govern one or more person's behavior or way of acting."

The class nodded in agreement.

"So then, if ethics are moral principles, who is to say what is right or wrong. Correct?" he asked. "Do I tell you what is right? Do your parents? Does the government? No. You tell *yourself* what is right and wrong."

A few students nodded their heads again. The professor continued his lecture as he walked up the stairs that led to the top level where Gabriel's desk was.

Then the professor turned and walked back down to his podium. "Hello students. I am Professor Alexander Pius. I was born in Edinburgh, but I was raised in different parts of Europe. Spain, Italy, and even parts of France. You may be able to tell by my accent, I spent my formative years in Madrid, in Spain. As many of you know, Europe has been a place of war and depravity ever since the first Transit. My childhood was a tumultuous time."

Gabriel was taking notes about where he said he was from. He wrote down *Why there is no history on him?* and circled it.

"Then I moved to London and finished my schooling. Graduated from Oxford with my degree in Psychology and then my masters in Para-psychology, focusing on the superhuman psyche." When he reached the bottom level, he paused. "I was fascinated by the idea of a human being with such power. The ability to move mountains or destroy cities. The power to cause destruction or bring about order. So, my question was, what is it that keeps us from, hmmm…let's say, overthrowing the world with our abilities?"

Gabriel sat upright. He knew there were several nations where powerful gifted individuals rose up and overthrew their country's government. Many of them had established dictatorships.

"Is it wrong to use one's own abilities to benefit themselves? Would it be wrong for someone to use their inherent skills to do well in their career?" the professor asked.

A female student raised her hand. The professor called on her. "I think it would be wrong for a gifted to use their ability to get ahead in the work force."

Professor Pius looked shocked by her answer. "So, would it be wrong for a more talented artist to sell more paintings than a less skilled one?"

The female student answered, "Well, no. I guess."

"Then why can't a gifted individual use their special abilities to succeed? It is the same thing, isn't it? Abilities are abilities, whether they are superhuman or not. We all have things that make us unique and special."

The female student sat silent, visibly interested.

"I greatly appreciate your answer," he said, giving a slight bow to the young lady. She blushed. Turning to the rest of the class, he asked, "Then you see my point? Are we not within our rights to use our gifts to make ourselves happy?"

Gabriel raised his hand. "But our gifts shouldn't just be used to fulfill our desires. That's dangerous, isn't it? Our goal is to help make the world a better place, not seek our selfish ends."

Realizing that he just said all of that out loud and in front of the whole class, Gabriel dropped his hand sheepishly.

"Well, it seems we have an unbeliever in our midst," Professor Pius said sarcastically. "If we all held onto such archaic ideals, no one would be able to rise above the rest and lead. We can't all be so naive...." He pulled up his tablet and thumbed through the roster, looking at the pictures. "Ah, Gabriel Green." He read his bio from the roster. "Grade B: Telekinetic," he said in a whisper. "Interesting."

The professor seemed to space out for a moment before composing himself and looking back at the class.

"Yes, well let's continue with the lecture," Professor Pius added.

For the remainder of class, the professor laid out the syllabus. He went over the assignments and various topics for the semester. As a sophomore, Gabriel knew that his work load would probably continue to grow. He took notes as Pius lectured on due dates and his policy for assignments.

At the end of class, Pius paused and looked around the room. "Now, my young minds eager for knowledge, for your first assignment, I want you to all use your ability in a way that makes you happy. Then document that experience in a short, one-page paper. This will be due next week."

The students looked at each other excitedly.

"Well, ladies and gentlemen, you have been an amazing class. I look forward to teaching you this semester. Class is dismissed."

Gabriel stood up to leave. He looked down at the Professor and saw him looking up. The glare from his glasses masked his eyes so Gabriel couldn't tell what he was looking at. A small group of students were already surrounding him to ask him questions. If nothing else, everyone in the class seemed to love this professor. *I guess I have to give him the benefit of the doubt*, he thought.

"Oh," Pius said, turning to face the crowds of students. "If anyone is interested in joining our discussion group, please take one of the fliers I have left at the doors."

Gabriel grabbed his bag and walked up the stairs to the exit, noticing the small table by the door. It had a stack of pamphlets about the professor's aforementioned discussion group. Students were grabbing them by the handful. Gabriel wondered to himself if this would be a good way to get closer to the professor.

FILE #06

THE BASICS

"There's no way your dad is Gideon Burns," Gabriel was saying as he rolled his eyes.

"I'm serious," Jake protested. "My dad runs The Burn Report website. He's the one who coined the term 'burning,' dude. I am telling you."

"So, your dad is the super lifestyle blogger and world traveler, Gideon Burns?" Gabriel said with some disbelief.

"Yes," Jake nodded. "I swear."

"How come you never told me before?"

"Well, it sounds weird sometimes opening with that. And honestly, I wanted people to get to know me for me. Not because my dad is a major internet celebrity."

As Gabriel held open the gymnasium door, Jake entered first. Gabriel shook his head in disbelief.

"You have to tell me about his article on New Eden. I want to go there so bad."

"Sure thing," Jake said. "I will tell you after our meeting."

Coach V corralled the team one of the team meeting rooms. Before the season was fully underway, he wanted to have a pre-season meeting. While they sat, Jake was explaining this to Gabriel. Jake gave him a reassuring punch on the shoulder and reminded him that he was picking things up quickly.

Gabriel's attention was pulled away when he heard someone nearby saying, "Somehow, Coach catches every mistake you make in a match. He's like a hawk, man. Nothing gets by him."

Gabriel sat next to Jake in the second-to-last row. After a few minutes, Jake realized Gabriel didn't know everyone's names so Jake introduced Gabriel to several of his teammates.

"This is Derek, Claudio, and you know Eames from the Sports Club," Jake said. Gabriel shook Derek's hand first and greeted him. Derek had an impressive grip and massively strong arms. His sleeveless shirt revealed dark-skinned arms that were thick and vascular.

Then Gabriel shook Claudio's hand, a portly Hawaiian kid with a mop of curly dark brown hair that looked just messy enough to have taken a long time to style. Afterwards, he waved to Eames. Eames was a speedster who oversaw the club. They had played a few times together in the Sports Club, but Gabriel didn't sign up this year as he was joining the Sparring Team.

Gabriel and Jake sat side-by-side at a white table, facing the large screen in the front. The screen was a thin board that allowed the user to write on it. Coach V looked like he was erasing the remains of whatever had been written on it before. Then he turned around and greeted the team.

"Very good, it seems everyone is here. Let's begin," he said in a somewhat-winded voice.

Coach looked around the room and made eye contact with Gabriel for a moment. "Well, for those of you who are new, this is the meeting room. We meet here very regularly. I believe that it's as important as it is to train diligently, it is also important to study and know your opponent. If you feel that training and power are the only means of growing with your ability, then you will not thrive using my system." Gabriel's eyes widened at that statement. Usually, Coach V wasn't so blatant. Then as if to answer Gabriel's concern, Coach added,

"Yes, that might be harsh. But I want you to understand that physical work and mental preparation are two very important parts of our training regimen. I feel it is only fair you understand what you're getting into from the beginning."

The room had an air of tension, but Gabriel nodded in agreement with Coach V.

"This room will be used in our post-meet follow-ups and for regular practices. Before any practice, we will be meeting here and discussing what practice will look like for the day. Any questions?"

"How many meets will we have this year?" asked one of the new teammates.

"We have eight," answered Coach V. "If we make it to the championships, then we'll have more."

Another one raised her hand and asked, "Have you decided who the starters will be yet?"

"Very good question. If you don't know, the team consists of eight starters. These are the fighters who will fight in our matches. We also have five substitutes. They will be used in a situation where a starter is injured, can't fight, or in case I decide to switch someone out. But to answer your question, no, I have not chosen all of the starters yet."

The next hand shot up. "Someone said that freshman don't start. Is that true?"

"It isn't a rule. However, I generally do not start my freshman because they are still learning about their gift. However, if a competitor came onto the team with significant control over their abilities, I would not be against starting them. That being said, I don't believe that is a common situation. Next question."

"How many schools do we usually compete against?" asked Claudio.

"We are in the eastern division, and there are ten schools with Gifted Departments that we will be competing against." Coach V looked around the room. No more hands were going up. So, he pulled out a few documents from his stack of papers.

"All right, everyone. Now that the initial questions have been answered, we will begin the qualification process for our starters and subs. Of the thirteen of you, eight will be starters and five will be subs."

Just then the back door opened, and Gabriel saw Assistant Coach Hu enter with a large box in her arms.

"Thank you, Jasmine. Perfect timing," Coach V said. "This brings me to our next order of business: uniforms."

Coach V took down names and handed out uniforms. A staff member with a unique gift was with them and had printed their names and numbers to the uniforms just by holding her hand out over the jersey. Gabriel remembered last semester where a similar gift was used in place of a printer to get his class schedule. When it was Gabriel's turn, he asked for number nine, which was his soccer team number. Luckily no one had taken it yet, and Gabriel walked away with his jerseys.

"You will notice that you have three jerseys. The navy blue one is our home jersey, the white with red is our away jersey, and the plain white and blue is our practice uniforms. Please wear those to our practices."

Coach V paused for a minute. Then he held up one of the jerseys, and a picture of one appeared on the screen behind him.

"Each jersey is made by a very unique gift that allows them to create materials that normally can't be made. This uniform is made by combining materials together in an amazing way. These uniforms will therefore provide you with a great deal of protection while you are in the ring. Outside of these protective uniforms, no other weapons, tools, or gear is allowed in the ring. Especially ones that would allow one to gain an advantage in the contest."

After some more explaining, Coach V ended by saying, "Well, now that we have explained all of that. I will be having the new members of the team working together and the advanced members working together."

So, with Coach V's direction, the squad moved out of the meeting room and into the arena. The main arena was a massive central room in the gymnasium, although it was only a room by definition. It was big enough to fit a football field inside it, and there was plenty of workout equipment to support the various teams on campus. Coach V had the freshman and sophomores in one group, and the juniors and seniors in another group.

In the beginners' group, Gabriel was surrounded by mostly students who looked much more confident than he felt. He noticed Jake standing in the far edge, looking unusually reserved. Before Gabriel could move to ask him why he looked upset, a hand grabbed his shoulder and spun him around.

"Hey, you made the team too! Congratulations!"

Gabriel's eyes were a blur for a moment. Then he saw Avery, who he met on the first day when Coach V had them running laps. Avery had reddish hair and a constant nonchalant. It was like nothing ever bothered him.

"Yeah, by the skin of my teeth," replied Gabriel.

"Good luck today," Avery said, patting Gabriel's shoulder. "Coach is known to run his team hard."

Coach V walked over to the group. "All right, ladies and gentlemen, today we are going to be pairing up and going over some basics."

He quickly began separating the beginners' group into pairs. Next, they were brought over to a stack of thick blue mats. Coach V then began demonstrating the proper stances for competition. Although Gabriel thought he knew how to stand, he quickly learned that his fighting stance was all wrong.

"Your stance is too narrow. You could easily be knocked off balance. Spread your legs wide, and you won't lose your balance. You have a defensive ability so you want to keep up a defensive stance." Coach showed Gabriel a wide stance to use, and Gabriel mirrored him. Then Coach moved toward Avery and also showed him an appropriate stance. Coach V spent most of that time showing the beginners proper stances for combat. He allowed the advanced members to work on some technical work.

Although Gabriel couldn't see much because he was working himself, in between attacks, he could see that Jin was leading them in a set of more advanced fighting techniques. Although Gabriel didn't really know Jin, but he had seen her sparring last year. She was graceful, poised, and, not to mention, fierce.

After about forty-five minutes of basic footwork, Gabriel and the team were called over. Once the team was around him again, Coach V said, "Next we will move into some basic combat techniques. Both the single and doubles matches are scored the same way."

"Who are our doubles team fighters?" Avery asked, interrupting Coach V.

Everyone's eyes widened. Even the rookies understood that you didn't just interrupt Coach V when he was talking. Avery clearly hadn't caught onto that fact.

Coach made a coughing noise in his throat and his eyes narrowed. "We haven't decided on that yet. Our last doubles team graduated back in May. So, we will be recruiting our new fighters this season." He paused for a moment. "Next time, wait until I am finished before interjecting."

Then Coach V looked around the room. Gabriel and Coach's eyes met. He gave Gabriel a look, but Gabriel didn't understand. Did Coach want him on the doubles team? But before he could even wonder what that look meant, Coach V continued his explanation of the point system.

"So, moving on, a sparring match is won by landing successful hits on your opponent. These can be physical punches or kicks or using your Gift. For each successful hit you land on your opponent, you receive a point and the same goes for your opponent. A match is won when ten points are earned, and you must win by two points."

All eyes were fixed on Coach V.

"Although points are the most common way to win a match, there are some alternate ways matches can be won. The first is if an opponent is knocked out. This match is called for the safety of the players, but it is not recommended. If a fighter wins too many matches this way, they can be suspended."

Gabriel noticed Coach V look in Lucien's direction.

"The second way is if a combatant is seriously injured. The match is called again for the safety of the fighters. But like I said before, if this happens a lot, and you are repeatedly hurting combatants, you can be suspended. The final way is if the referee feels that a match is one-sided. They will call the fight so the losing combatant is not harmed."

As Coach scanned the room, he looked at his eight new recruits. The majority of them were freshman, except for Gabriel. Many of them were unskilled with their abilities, but most of them had potential. One stood out of that group of new recruits. His gaze stopped on Gabriel.

"So, because points can be easily earned by landing a punch or a kick, we will be having Jin Kenichi come up and show us a few good ways to land some quick hits in for an effective win."

Coach V stepped to the side and started clapping. The group did so as well while Jin made his way to the front of the room. Gabriel noticed that Lucien was clapping but also rolling his eyes.

"For this exercise, I want you to mirror my motions," instructed Jin. "We will be going over proper combat techniques. These are some ways to delivers blows to your opponent."

Jin moved into a martial arts stance. Her legs were spread apart and locked. Her heels hovered over the ground just slightly. Strong yet loose, her body was an example of perfect posture, all the better to move in for a strike or to dodge an attack. Jin showed them how to deliver a punch while keeping balance. This way they could move into a defensive stance or continue attacking.

Then Jin instructed the new recruits on some effective movement strategies for delivering a kick and taught them proper footwork when moving, attacking, and defending. With her instruction, the newbies learned about pacing and the flow of an effective punch. Jin focused on footwork as she did on punching. According to her, footwork was more important than physical strength.

All the while, Gabriel was remembering the battle with Drake. He realized how little fighting experience he had at that moment and when he had fought Drake. He was lucky he was to have survived that encounter.

After she felt that she had effectively explained everything, Jin called an end to practice.

Gabriel moved over to the stands where he kept his duffle bag. He grabbed his water bottle and took a long drink. Then he dropped it into his bag and wiped his face with his towel and looked over at what the advanced fighters were doing. Lucien seemed to be leading the group, still pushing those team members. He looked like a drill sergeant.

He was having the advanced group attack a set of targets with their gifts. Gabriel saw him get really close to a teammate he didn't recognize. He seemed to be angry at them for not hitting the target. Just as Coach V came over, he backed away. A pulse of emotion struck Gabriel, a mix of anger and resentment.

Just then, Gabriel noticed that Jake wasn't with the group. He was behind them, doing push-ups, possibly excluded for something he did or a punishment for not doing it right. Either way, Gabriel didn't like the way Lucien was running things.

Coach V called the team to come over. He had a stack of forms in his hand. He held them up in the air. When everyone was around him, he called out, "These are the schedules for the season. Keep in mind, they are not final yet. Sometimes we manage to schedule an extra meet here or there, and sometimes a meet falls through because of different issues. So, keep that in mind. All right? Now, before we dismiss for the evening, I wanted to let everyone know that Simon Cruz has agreed to be my assistant manager. He will cover scheduling practices and much of the other data analysis for the team. Because of his gift, he will be a huge asset to the team."

FILE #07

THE OTHER INTERN

As the team began to clear out of the arena, Gabriel told Jake that he needed to speak with Coach V for a bit. He waved goodbye to Jake and walked over to the Coach, who was speaking with Simon. When Gabriel approached them, he asked if he could speak with Coach V.

"Oh, I'll get out of your way." Simon nodded and then asked Coach V, "Do you need anything else?"

"No," he answered. "But actually, can Simon come with us? I have him working on this case as well."

Gabriel looked around the room and nodded in approval.

Coach V left the arena and headed to his office. Gabriel and Simon packed up and followed. As the two boys walked down the hallway, Gabriel nudged Simon. "Hey, I wanted to ask you something."

"What's that?" he asked.

"I feel like we need to meet for real."

"What do you mean?" Simon asked.

"I feel like I don't know you. I know the pretend Simon that you were pretending to be while you were undercover. But I want to meet the real Simon, all right?"

"The real Simon..."

"Yeah, the guy that we saw down in the laboratory last semester. Who was that guy?"

"Oh, I guess I can be pretty singularly focused when I am on a mission. I think when I have a mission, something to focus on, that's when I feel more like myself."

"So, that's the real you, huh?" Gabriel asked. "Is that why you tried to help Jake with his gift right away?"

"I supposed so. Well, fine then." Simon put out his hand out, and Gabriel took it. The two shook hands. Simon's motion was a little jolted and stiff while Gabriel's was lax.

"Nice to meet you, Simon Cruz."

"It's nice to meet you, Gabriel Green."

"How about tomorrow, you and I get coffee and we get to know each other for real?" asked Gabriel.

"That sounds good," Simon said.

"There is a concert coming up in a few weeks. Do you want to get the group together and go?" asked Gabriel as they walked.

"Totally. I tutored one of the band members last semester. I could get us tickets pretty easily."

"That'd be awesome."

Back in Coach V's office, Gabriel and Simon sat at the two seats across from V's desk. Coach V stood behind the desk and faced the two young men. He set up the small device that he used last time. Once he did so, he said, "So, Gabriel, let me catch you up to speed."

Gabriel didn't realize he wasn't up to speed. He thought he had the information, but apparently there was more to this than he understood.

"Simon has been working on this case for some time. He was our mole in the science department last semester and he was tasked with finding out where our information leak was."

"Information leak?" Gabriel asked.

"Yes, as it turns out, Drake was sharing secrets with some unknown third party. Then after you and Jake intervened, we moved in to bust him. Simon has remained on campus as a student-intern in the science department, and in an attempt to keep up his cover, we asked him to work with me in the sparring team."

"So, what is his role now?" Gabriel asked.

"His role isn't much different than it was before. He is looking for the information leak's target. He is searching all digital means and trying to find where Drake was sending his information."

Gabe turned to Simon. "Have you found anything?"

"Unfortunately, no. Because his gift gives him superhuman mental power, he didn't need to use much in the way of online resources."

"So, is it a dead end?"

"It's hard to say, but my job is to search every nook and cranny of Drake's database until I can say one way or the other. Once I have fully explored everything online, then we can examine his laboratory for physical clues."

Coach turned to Gabriel. "That's where you come in, Gabriel. What have you found out in Professor Pius' class?"

"Well, he definitely has some, uh, unique views on gifts. But he does have an after-school discussion group," Gabriel answered, pulling out the flier from class.

He showed Simon and Coach the form. It was printed in a large font that listed the title of the group, when and where they met, and said that Professor Pius led the discussions. Simon scanned it over and then handed it to Coach V.

"This discussion group of his meets in the Old Cottage," Simon said with a confused expression. "Isn't that building closed for renovations?"

Coach V nodded. "It was, to my knowledge, but maybe Pius got the board's approval to meet there when work wasn't being done?"

"Why would he want to meet that far away from the main campus? That building is off toward the forest near the north wall."

"Maybe he doesn't want anyone accidentally stumbling into one of his meetings," Coach V said. "If it were a classroom or a lecture hall, someone might be able to listen in on him."

Gabriel nodded. He had never seen the building, and honestly, he wasn't even sure where it was. He was glad that Coach V and Simon did.

"Want me to sneak in and see what I can find out?" asked Gabriel.

"No," said Coach V. "Well, not sneak in, that is. I don't think that will be necessary."

"So, you think that we're on the right track. What about the other two suspects?"

"I think we can pretty much cross those two off of our list of suspects. Simon and I have checked them out. Right, Simon?" Coach asked.

Simon nodded. "I am confident that they are not involved in this case."

"So, that means Pius is our guy?" asked Gabriel.

"That would seem to be the case. However, until we have some real evidence, our Organization can't act. As you know, 'innocent until proven guilty' is the law."

Gabriel nodded. "So, Coach V, that brings up a question I have. What's the organization you work for?"

Coach furrowed his eyebrows for a moment, as if he wasn't sure about the answer. His puzzled expression made Gabriel unsure if he understood the question. Then Coach looked at Gabriel. "I guess there really is no reason to keep it from you."

"Oh, well, if I can't know, then I understand. I guess."

"No, I suppose it is time. Gabriel Green, you are the newest disciple in the Guild. The Guild is the agency where Simon and I really work."

Gabriel mouthed the word *Guild* a few times without actually making a sound. "That's the greatest agency name I have ever heard of."

Coach V smirked. "Well, now back to the mission at hand."

"You were saying, you wanted us to acquire some hard evidence on Professor Pius," Simon said very matter-of-factly.

"Oh, yeah, of course. So, uh, I will go to Prius' next discussion group. Right?" Gabriel asked.

"Yes, but I don't want you to go in alone."

Gabriel looked at Simon. "Awesome, I think Simon and I can handle it," he said, elbowing Simon's arm.

"No," Coach said with a small chuckle. "Not Simon. Simon isn't an intern. Well, he was pretending to be a college intern, but he isn't an agency intern."

"Wait, there's another intern?" Gabe asked.

"Yes, of course. You will be joined by Serena."

FILE #08

THE GHOST

"Wait, Serena's an intern?" asked Gabriel.

Coach V nodded. "Yes, of course. She was on our radar long before you were, Gabriel."

"Wow, I didn't even think about it. But I guess that makes a lot of sense."

Simon looked at Coach. "So, should I continue to do my data sweeps and see if I can find a target for the leaks?"

"Yes. Well, this was a good meeting. Gabriel, I want you to meet up with Serena and tell her what you're going to be doing. I will get in touch with her mentor and give her the intelligence we have so far."

"Who's her mentor?"

"That's on a need-to-know basis, Gabriel. In our business, no one person gets to know all of the information. Unfortunately, the Guild is still hurting from the situation with Drake. And we are keeping all sensitive information on a need-to-know basis."

"I understand," Gabriel said.

Simon left while Gabriel grabbed his bag. He threw it over his shoulder and made for the door, but Coach V called to him.

"Oh, Gabriel, I wanted to tell you something."

"What's that, Coach?"

"I am very excited to be working with you. I have been waiting for this day for a long time."

"You have?" Gabriel asked.

"Yes, I have. Do you remember the day I first met you? That was not only a school recruitment but to see if you might be a good fit for our team. I am just glad we got to you before another agency realized your potential."

Gabriel's face turned red slightly. He nodded and thanked Coach V for his vote of confidence. Leaving the office, he made his way for his room. A wave of exhaustion suddenly washed over him.

***

That night, Gabriel was awoken by several masked people standing around him. All of them were dressed in black shirts and black pants, and each had a black ski mask over their faces. The menacing look would be complete if it wasn't for the poor job they did in cutting out the eyeholes in their masks. One in particular was so off that he had to constantly readjust his mask so he could see.

One of them stepped forward. His thick accent made it apparent it was Lucien. He said, "Stand, Gabriel Green. You will be tested on this night."

Gabriel stood up. In his shorts and T-shirt, he felt the chill of the night air. Two people grabbed him and a third threw a black bag over his face to obstruct his vision. They pulled him up and practically carried him out of the room.

A thought hit him. *Where was Jake?* He realized that one of the masked figures must have been Jake. Otherwise, they never would have been able to get into the locked dorm room. He huffed. In the end, it was all in good fun.

They crept through the halls, careful not to wake the resident assistant. Quietly, they pushed through the doors and into the cool, brisk evening air. Gabriel didn't know what time it was, but they dragged him through the grass, soaking his legs in dew.

He wasn't sure where they were headed, but based on the ground, he guessed they were going through the main courtyard. Then the ground changed from grass to concrete. He picked up his feet to keep from scraping them. In his mind's eye, he pictured where the walkway led. From his estimation, he guessed they were now nearing the library.

All of a sudden, there were bright lights. Even through the black bag, the light was noticeable. It must have meant they were inside now. He guessed they were near the library, but he wasn't sure where exactly they were. Maybe the inside library itself or even the science building.

After some more movement, Gabriel could feel the change in levels. They are carrying him upstairs. After a quick turn, they went up another flight. Then another. After a few moments, they were on the third floor. *No, the fourth floor*, he thought.

The group stopped. Gabriel was holding his breath for whatever crazy task was going to be asked of him. Then he heard the sound of a thick lock clicking in front of him. They passed through a room. The anticipation was starting to eat away at his nerves. The waiting was worse than whatever they were going to make him do.

Then all of the hustle stopped. All of a sudden, they dropped him to the ground like a dumbbell. He felt dusty, wooden floorboards underneath him. A solid layer of filth covered the floor like a blanket. His hands felt the cold floor and his bare legs brushed against the dirt and grime.

Someone ripped the mask off his face and his eyes tried to adjust to the room. It was dark. Almost completely dark. However, a single light source in the distance helped the room make sense. He saw the figures all around him. Then he realized he wasn't the only victim tonight. Another figure stood beside him. To his shock, a third was beside them and shaking.

Three subjects of this hazing. Gabriel readied himself for whatever was to happen next. The second victim had his mask removed as well. Gabriel recognized him as his eyes adjusted. It was Avery. They remove the third victim's mask. It was a girl named Zoey that he knew from his earliest days on campus. He didn't even know she made the team.

One of the ski-masked men stepped forward. He pointed to the source of the light. They looked in that direction. Beside the small, flickering light was a tall, standing mirror. The layer of dust over it made it impossible to see a reflection.

The masked man spoke. "Which of you will summon the ghost?"

No one moved. The crew dressed in all black picked up all three teammates and moved them closer to the mirror and then dropped them once again. Gabriel could see patterns in the dust. There was a handprint on the mirror that had a thinner layer of dust over it. *Others have been brought here before.* He could see foot and hand prints in the dust on the floor in front of the mirror.

This time, a girl barked orders. Gabriel could tell that it was Katrina. "Summon the ghost!" she yelled.

Looking at the other two, Gabriel decided to take the challenge. Not believing in ghosts, Gabriel expected this must be some sort of trial. A test of bravery maybe. So, he stood up. A mess of dirt clung to his legs. He stepped forward, and all the kidnappers moved aside.

A low-volume chanting of "hoo, hoo, hoo, hoo" began as he walked closer. As he stopped inches from the mirror, the chanting hushed to a slight whisper. He placed a hand on the mirror. With his other hand, he brushed the layer of dust and grit. His tired expression stared back at him. He passed his hand over the mirror again, showing his shoulders and stomach. Next, he swiped up and down.

Staring at the mirror for several seconds, Gabriel waited for something to happen. It would seem that cleaning the mirror wasn't enough. He looked back and the group all nodded at him. One of them made a motion with his hand, giving him the signal to continue. So, he turned back with a sigh and looked at the mirror.

He looked at the mirror and called out, "Ghost, I want you to show yourself to me." Nothing happened. Waiting for a few more seconds, Gabriel didn't expect any sort of reaction. Several more seconds of dead silence lingered in the air. Again, he turned and looked at the group behind him.

Then he noticed something out of the corner of his eye. Quickly, he swung back to the mirror and a strange fuzzy figure appeared. A few moments later, it began to take shape in the form of a human's silhouette. Then the features became clearer. It was an old man. At least he was pretty sure it was. He looked at Gabriel with cold eyes. Gabriel felt like his body temperature dropped.

His eyes widened and his jaw dropped. "Wh-what in the name of Venus?!"

"Leave me alone!" the ghostly apparition screamed. "I told you to never come here again!"

Gabriel screamed, "I'm sorry!" as he ran back to the group. All of them scattered and ran. They rushed through the halls until they reached the front doors and stumbled into the quad.

The whole group panted as they all stopped there, doubled over. Gabriel was panting, feeling like he had never run so quickly in his life. He stood huddled over with his head between his legs, gasping for air. Avery sat on the cold, wet grass beside him.

Then a voice came from behind them. "Well done, Gabriel. You showed courage up there."

Gabriel turned and looked at the speaker. "What in the name of Venus was that thing?" he asked.

"A myth. A legend. A ghost?" she suggested. "We can't be sure. No one's gone up there long enough to find out. But tradition is what brings us up there once a year."

Gabriel could tell that the one before him was Jin. Her calming tone. The way she spoke with her cadence. He was certain it was Jin. And for some reason, that calmed him. If it was another, Gabriel might have lost his temper after such a dangerous excursion. But somehow, Jin's presence made him feel like everything was under control.

"So, are we done here?" he asked the group.

"Can we go home now?" asked Avery, still on the ground.

"Yes, you are free to go now," yelled another masked voice. "But you two have to run one hundred laps tomorrow for not accepting the challenge. Gabriel, you are exempt."

Gabe rolled his eyes at the masked man that he knew was Lucien.

"Have a good night," Lucien said and turned to walk away.

FILE #09

The Underground

That following week, Gabriel planned to meet up with Serena and head for Professor Pius' discussion group. For the last few days, Gabriel had had a strange feeling in the pit of his stomach. It started once he learned that Serena was also training to work for the agency. Gabriel didn't know that she was even interested in becoming an agent. He had thought her biggest passion was music. Apparently, he didn't know her as well as he thought.

Then again, he wasn't able to tell anyone about his involvement in the agency either. So, maybe he didn't have any right to be upset. He sat at the water fountain in the center of campus, near the quad. The sun was just beginning to hide behind the edges of the mountains. He pulled his device out of his pocket to check the time, and see if Simon gave him any updates. It was almost six so Serena would be arriving any minute now.

Gabriel continued to scroll through his phone to pass the time. It helped keep his mind off the anxious feeling in his chest.

He read a few headlines on a news page.

The Prime Minister of Germania decrees new act to protect the empire.

New Energy Company seeks to power all of South America before the end of the year.

It wasn't working. The anxiety in his chest was killing him. He got up and walked around the water fountain five, six, seven times. Maybe more. He lost count. Finally, Serena came around the student union building into view. Gabriel nodded to her and walked in her direction.

"Hey," he said, noticeably awkward.

"Hi," she answered, raising an eyebrow. "Are you all right?"

"Sure thing," he replied. "Let's head toward the Old Cottage. We can talk on the way."

They made their way away from the quad and toward the oldest building on campus.

Once the crowd thinned out a little, Gabriel whispered, "So, you are interning at the Guild too?"

"I am. My…uh…stepdad is in the Guild, and he wanted me to follow in his footsteps. Well, he actually didn't at first. But when I told him that I wanted to, he claimed that it was his idea."

"Really?" Gabriel asked, surprise showing on his face as well as in his voice.

"You never asked, Gabriel. That's why I never told you," she said, answering the question that Gabriel wanted to ask but hadn't.

"I…I know."

"You didn't tell me you were either," she said.

"That's true. I honestly didn't know for sure I wanted to be an agent. I mean, I grew up with all the old heroes as every other kid. Lionheart, Diviner, Glass, they were some of my favorite agents growing up. Every kid grew up kind of wanting to be them. I just never thought I *could* ever be like them."

Serena touched Gabriel's arm. "You can be, okay?"

Immediately, he blushed. But he told himself it was just the comment, not her touch. Then Gabriel nodded in reply.

After a moment of silence, Serena said, "So, before we get there, maybe we should run over the mission?"

"Yeah."

"My mentor said this is an information-gather mission only. We aren't starting anything because we don't have any evidence that Pius is really our guy yet. Once we get some intelligence, we can return to our respective mentors and report what we find out," Serena said with some authority. "All right?"

"That's exactly what mine told me too. But mine also added not to do anything stupid."

"I thought that was a given?"

"I guess it should be, huh?" Gabriel joked.

They went over some of the finer details before they got anywhere near the building. When the two would-be agents arrived at the Old Cottage, they noticed a small group of students at the entrance. They were all being ushered into the building. Except for one. Gabriel stopped when Serena grabbed him.

When they approached the front door, the young woman that was outside asked them what they were there for. Gabriel was about to answer when Serena said they were there for the discussion group. She told her that both of them were in Pius' class.

She looked at them with a tinge of suspicion. "All right, head inside. Watch out for the tools and equipment. They're doing some renovation work inside."

As they entered, Gabriel noticed the room smelled like sawdust and paint. It was very obvious that work was still being done in this room. It was so bad that it was actually hard to breathe.

"Why would they meet here?" asked Gabriel in a soft voice.

"I don't know really. But my mentor thinks that it is odd that he even got permission to meet here. What with all of the work going on. It is very suspicious to me."

"How so?"

"Well, it's so far from the rest of campus, for one thing. Next, just getting permission must have taken either some very good persuasion or he bribed the school board," Serena answered. "This place has to be a safety hazard."

"That makes sense." They followed the signs that led them down into a basement.

Serena opened the door. "Let's just see what we can learn tonight. We'll talk afterwards about our theories."

When they got to the bottom of the stairs, there was a sign that said, *Welcome to The Underground*. It was an intricately-carved wooden sign with a beautiful walnut varnish. There were a lot more kids down here than either of them expected. It was a large basement that was mostly furnished and could hold about a hundred students. There was a small stage in the front where Pius stood, talking with a few students. In front of the stage were rows of chairs facing Pius.

Most of the rows were full, but Gabriel saw a few empty ones in the back. The two quickly slid into their seats and waited for the meeting to begin. Although they weren't hiding, they wanted to be able to sneak out if they needed. Blending into the crowd would be their best bet.

Within a few moments, Pius stood at the top of the stage and looked out at all of the students. He smiled in a way that looked like he was genuinely happy to see all of them. Then he spoke in that silky-smooth voice of his. "Welcome, everyone. It is wonderful to see you all again. I am so glad that you all have decided to return. And it looks like we have a few more faces."

As he spoke, Gabriel noticed that Serena's eyes were sparkling like they did when she used her gift. He wasn't sure what she was doing, but he didn't want to interrupt her.

"Last time, we had people share some of their feelings on their gifts. Some people were bold enough to share what they wanted to get out of life because of their gifts. It was a moving night, if I do say so myself. I feel like you all teach me more than I teach you."

Then he started clapping. The whole crowd followed suit and soon there was a standing ovation. Gabriel knew that Coach V didn't trust Pius, but honestly, he found it hard not to like him. He was so cheerful and kind. Gabriel found himself thinking how much he enjoyed listening to him speak.

Pius continued to speak to the crowd about how much of a blessing a person's gift is to them. How they should be grateful, and how they should use their gift to make them happy. Gabriel noticed that much of the crowd were enthused about his speech.

After a few minutes, Pius started having students come up and talk about how thankful they were for Pius and the Underground, which appeared to be what this group called themselves. The students were all talking about how Pius created a space for them to talk and feel accepted.

After the fourth students went, Pius came back to the stage. He spoke for several more minutes about the importance of their gifts. How they would be important in the days to come. The whole crowd watched intently and they listened with bated breath.

"Everyone, thank you for coming tonight. This is your family now. We are all a family. I will lead each of you into bigger and better things. Will you follow me into that wide-open world?"

The crowd began to cheer. Gabriel followed suit, standing to cheer for Pius. Serena noticed him standing with an odd look. *What is he doing?* she wondered. She stood slowly and started clapping as well. She wasn't sure if Gabriel was really interested, but she wanted to blend into the crowd as best as she could.

Pius spoke for a few more minutes on the idea of family that he presented. He often referred to himself as their father figure.

He even said he was their guide a few times. Serena wasn't sure what was going on, but she wasn't sure she bought into Pius being their leader.

At the end of his speech, Pius said, "Farewell my children and have a goodnight."

Then he rushed off of the stage and found himself in a crowd of students, who bombarded him with questions. Serena began tugging at Gabriel's shirt, telling him it was time to go. He followed, but he watched Pius' reactions. As he watched, he saw Pius was shaking hands, thanking students for attending, and taking a genuine interest in the kids around him.

Meanwhile, Serena used her telepathic gift to keep anyone from seeing them so they could sneak out. She had used this same ability when they faced Dr. Drake. Serena made an agent who was looking for Gabriel not perceive that he was still there. She did so by manipulating his brain's interpretation of what it was seeing.

***

Outside, Gabriel and Serena regrouped when they made it safely out of sight. Serena was the first to ask what Gabriel thought of the situation.

"I honestly don't see what this guy could be up to," Gabriel said.

"I don't either, but there are some odd things going on." As they walked back toward campus, she continued, "Well, first of all, I didn't notice direct mind control, but there was something going on in the heads of the students there. I can't put my finger on it for sure."

"So, you're thinking there's some kind of mind control going on?" he asked.

"Yes, something along those lines. But I will talk to my mentor when we get back."

Gabriel nodded. "Me too." He thought for a moment. "Who is your mentor?"

"Technically, I'm not allowed to tell you yet. Didn't your mentor tell you that?" Serena asked, unsure as to why he would ask.

"Oh, right. Coa- I mean cool. My mentor did mention that," he said.

Serena smirked. "Listen, basically, this is what we know." She held up her index finger. "Number one: Pius is meeting in the Old Cottage off on the far side of campus. How he got access to it during its renovation is anyone's guess. Two: He is definitely using something on his students, but I don't know what yet. And three: The students are all fawning over him. He has them eating out of his hands."

Gabriel nodded at each point.

"So, I think all of those point to some kind of mental manipulation going on here," she said.

"This just went from bad to worse." Gabriel sighed.

FILE #10

THE MEET

The following week was one of the more strenuous weeks of Gabriel's life. Although he had played soccer in high school, Coach V ran a much tighter training routine. As their first meet approached, the team continued their workout routine.

Gabriel was noticeably out of shape. Whereas most of the regular teammates worked out year-round, Gabriel hadn't worked out as regularly since high school. So, he knew he had some extra work to get caught up.

For two straight weeks, Gabriel focused as much as he could on preparing for the meet. He continued his classes, homework, and keeping an eye on Professor Pius, however, for the moment, nothing was quite as important as preparing for the meet. When that Saturday arrived, Gabriel was as excited as could be.

The team had to wake up extremely early that morning. Jake and Gabriel awoke and were ready to go before the sun was up. As they left, Gabriel noticed that he was notably more excited than Jake.

Before he could say anything, Jake asked, "What are you so excited for?"

"Well, we are going to our first sparring meet. I haven't competed in one before, so I'm pretty excited to give it a go."

"You know we won't even compete, right?"

Gabriel nodded. "Yeah, that's probably true. But it's still a cool experience."

"Why do you always look at the bright side?"

Gabriel paused for a moment. "I don't know. Someone has to."

The two walked the rest of the way in silence. Gabriel didn't know what to say. He understood Jake's apprehension and mindset. Jake was a competitor, an athlete. Jake was a fighter, and he loved the sparring team. So, to ride the bench again was something of a slap in the face for somehow who had usually been at the top of every physical sport he tried.

When they met the rest of the team outside of the gymnasium, Gabriel heard someone ask, "Do you know how we're getting there?"

"We are being teleported, of course. Don't you pay attention?" Katrina snapped.

"I know that, but who is teleporting us?"

"The college hires someone from the Nimbus Teleportation Service to get us there," he answered while staring at his tablet.

Coach V came out through the entrance and asked Simon, "Are we ready to go?"

Gabriel noticed a woman was with him. *That must be the person from the teleportation company.*

"We are, sir," Simon answered.

"Good," Coach replied. "Everyone, this is our teleportation expert. I want you to listen to her instructions very carefully, all right?"

The students all nodded their heads and some answered aloud. The lady walked to the center and began giving instructions.

"My name is Claire. I will be teleporting you to the meet. Are you all excited?" she asked and waited for replies. A few students replied with cheery whoops and yells.

"It's too early to be excited about anything!" Jake exclaimed.

"So, the first thing to remember is to hold your breath when I tell you to do so. In the moment before we teleport and the moment we come out the other side, there will be no oxygen, so you might hyperventilate. It's safer to hold your breath until we come through, all right?"

She spent the next ten minutes or so going over what she wanted them to do, how to stand, and other safety protocols. When everyone was standing in a tight circle with their arms all interlocked and facing her, she started.

The moment that she counted to three, Gabriel immediately held his breath. He closed his eyes, like she asked, and felt a sensation like his body was being pulled by invisible forces in every direction. Then he noticed the light all around him getting sucked from the area. All of a sudden, there was nothing. Just complete blackness. Even his senses seemed gone. But just as quick as the nothingness came, it was replaced by a symphony of sound. All around them were people with headsets, calling orders and screaming questions. He was almost blinded by the sheer brightness of the area.

When Gabriel's eyes adjusted, he realized it wasn't actually that bright, but it was the change from being in complete darkness that shocked his eyes so much. The room was like a landing zone for teams coming from around the country. There were large circles set up with white paint, their landing pads. As they exited their landing pad, he saw three more teams teleport into the large room. A large cloud symbolled banner was hanging near the wall that said, *Nimbus Teleportation: Getting You There Now.*

It took a decent amount of time before Gabriel's senses were completely back to normal. Then he noticed that the room was a basketball arena and the team's banners around the top level. There was large arena seating that stretched up what seemed like a mile.

A woman in a headset approached them and directed the team down a large hallway. They went into a backroom and into another hallway. Before they realized it, the team was outside and being directed to another arena. Gabriel craned his neck to hear the woman's directions. He couldn't hear because when they exited the building, they were pushed into a massive crowd of people all heading toward the stadium as well.

He saw Simon and Coach V nodding to her, and the team started moving through the crowd toward the building. While the crowd was going one direction, Coach V led the team through a different path toward the back of the stadium. When they approached, they were checked into their locker room and were given lockers to put their gear. Gabriel noticed tons of guards at every hallway and a bunch of people in black and white referee shirts. He had no idea this was what it was like on this side of the event.

Inside, the coach began going over the plan for the meet. Each of the teams were going to be sorted into brackets to compete against one another. After the eight competitors fought, there would be a single winner. That winner went on to the next round. The winning school would be decided based on who had the most points from their successive rounds.

When the first match for S.I.A was called, Gabriel was chosen to be the substitute. He walked behind Lucien, who was side-by-side with Coach V. Although Coach V was giving him directions and pointers, Lucien didn't seem to be listening. Gabriel noticed him glance in his direction right before they entered the main arena. His expression was a mix of cockiness and nonchalance. Gabriel knew Lucien thought he was better than everyone else, but even this was a little much.

"Ready to see a show?" he whispered to Gabriel as they went through the double doors.

Before he could answer, they were met with the sound of applause and screaming. The stands were practically erupting with cheers and jeers. He could see the different colors for the four schools in the stands. It seemed the home team, Athens, had the most present. But he saw some wearing the navy blue and red S.I.A colors here and there.

The team sat down at a bench beside a large ring. Gabriel instantly noticed the fighting ring. These were similar in shape to the octagonal rings back at school, but these ones didn't have the black metal fencing around them. Instead, these had glass walls. Upon closer inspection, Gabriel noticed some unique hexagonal patterns on the glass, so faint they were almost imperceptible.

Simon stopped beside Gabriel. "Noticing the new model?" he asked.

"Yeah," Gabriel answered. "I've never seen a sparring ring like this one before."

"Yeah, they are supposed to be the newest thing in gift nullification. You see that honeycomb-like pattern on the glass?"

Gabriel nodded.

"Those patterns are supposedly made with an infused Venisium chemical. The stuff is experimental, I hear."

"Wow, I can't believe this stuff actually can keep the energy from people's powers contained. It's pretty impressive, if you ask me," Gabriel said.

Coach V was waving the two boys over. The coach wanted Gabriel to sit next to him so he could explain the progression of the fight. Zoey sat down next to him. Coach had chosen Zoey to be the other sub. Gabriel noticed she had a streak of pink in her hair this week. It was usually something colorful. Someone told him she was from New Eden in Africa, but he didn't get to ask her where yet.

His mind was starting to race because of the anticipation of the fight, so he tried to reign in his mind as best he could. Gabriel looked over and saw Simon sitting on the far side of the bench. The two nodded at each other as the fight began.

Lucien made his way up the steps into the ring. The massive octagonal shaped ring was bathed in lights. The blackish pillars at each corner were the only part that obscured the viewers vision, but for the most part the entire ring was visible. Coach V pulled Gabriel in as he put his arm on his shoulder.

"Now, I want you to watch the match closely. Lucien may be brash, boastful, and even a little condescending, but he is a great competitor," Coach V said over the din of the crowd.

Gabriel nodded in reply. "You got it, sir."

The referee entered behind Lucien's competitor. The opponent was a large boy with thick arms and legs. His coffee-colored skin was mildly damp as he entered the ring. At first Gabriel thought it was sweat. But once the match started, he realized it was something else.

The referee called both boys into the center of the ring. A large circle was in the center of the ring. Gabriel couldn't hear what the ref was saying, but Coach explained she was explaining the basics. They usually reminded the fighters about fouls, penalties, and other illegal aspects of the competition.

When the fight began, the combatant summoned a large orb of water. All of that moisture on his skin was pulled into the air and formed the sphere in front of him. Instantly, Gabriel realized that the water wasn't sweat, it was part of his gift.

Coach V leaned in toward Gabriel. "Now, Lucien should have an advantage in this match."

Gabriel asked why.

"Well, with his electric strike, that young man is more susceptible to getting shocked with all of that water."

Gabriel's eyes widened. "Oh, that makes sense. So, you think Lucien will win easily?"

Coach V didn't answer right away. He seemed to be weighing his words. Finally, he answered, "Well, maybe. I don't think any fight is completely one-sided. However, the ranking has him against the eighth seed on his team. So, the odds are in Lucien's favor all around."

Inside the ring, the fighters were dancing around each other. It was several seconds before the first blows were struck. Lucien threw several punches at the young man, but he used his water orb to block the attacks. Every time, Lucien got splashed with water. However, Lucien was able to land the first blow and received a point.

When the combat began again, Lucien was right back on top of the youth. Lucien had an intense, oppressive fighting style. He didn't let up. Instantly, he scored a second and third point for himself. Finally, the water manipulator, whose name was Dawit, was able to get some space between himself and Lucien. He threw the orb of water at him and doused Lucien. At that point, Lucien was using his electricity to cover his hands. When the water covered him, he was instantly shocked by his own gift.

Lucien fell to the ground. The referee approached to make sure he was okay, but Lucien sprang to one knee. The referee called for a point for Dawit. Lucien grew enraged. He shot a look of rage at the ref and punched the ground.

Unfortunately, this was a swing in the fight. Lucien was so enraged with losing a point that he made short work of Dawit. He scored seven unanswered points and won the fight in just a few short minutes. The referee warned Lucien at the end of the fight that his aggression was noted, and if he didn't calm down, he would be given a technical foul.

Lucien brushed the referee off and left the ring with a smirk on his face. He turned and walked to Coach V, who was standing there looking very stern and disapproving. He pulled Lucien aside and spoke with him while the rest of the team was ushered to their next match.

Several other matches began over the next few hours. Jin competed in a quickly-won victory, as did Katrina. However, both Derek and Claudio lost their matches. But in the end, it would be the match that never happened that had the most impact on the team.

FILE #11
THE SUBSTITUTE

When Gabriel was brought over to observe the next match as a substitute, the whole team was looking for Eames. Everyone was confused because the fight was supposed to be starting. Eames's competitor was already in the ring, looking somewhat perturbed.

Gabriel was just going to help the team look when Simon and Avery came rushing over to the group. They immediately walked over to Coach V and told him what happened.

As it turned out, Eames was zipping around the locker room with his gift. When he exited and rounded a corner, he slipped on some water and went careening into a wall. A medical team was looking at him as they spoke. They told Coach that the initial prognosis was a broken ankle.

One of the teammates asked, "Isn't there a gifted medic that could heal him?"

Coach shook his head. "They might be able to mend the bone, but he would still be out of competition for some time while he healed. Even after you set a bone and it begins to heal, you still need to rest for weeks or it could re-break."

"Plus, these medics aren't miracle workers. They can't magically make his bone be not broken," Simon added.

Everyone nodded.

Just then, a referee approached the group. He told them that they had just a matter of seconds before they were going to have to forfeit the match. The referee explained that the rules dictated that if a substitute cannot be found in the allotted time, the team would be required to forfeit, and the points would be awarded to the other team.

Coach V's eyes shot to Gabriel. In the crowd of people, he was the only one who could do it. "Gabriel, I need you to sub in for Eames. Otherwise, we lose the fight."

"What, me?" Gabriel asked. "What about Jake or Zoey?"

"Zoey's ability would be at a distinct disadvantage in this fight. Her competitor has ice manipulation. Jake would be the clear choice, but he's currently across the arena subbing for another match."

Simon interjected, "We have exactly thirty-nine seconds before the referee calls this match, and we forfeit. There's no time for him to get here."

"That means the other school would get a solid ten points, and we would get none. That would give them a huge advantage over the rest of the schools."

Gabriel looked around. Simon looked at him with a determined expression. He wasn't sure, but he thought he saw a flicker of a smile for a split second.

"All right, let's do it."

Coach led him over to the ring and the referee checked him into the fight. He called both boys over to the center of the ring. He looked at them both and explained that he wanted to see a clean fight. Excessive aggression would not be tolerated. He told them that they would be watched, and no illegal activity would be allowed. Then he asked them if they understood. First, Michael, his competitor, nodded his head. Gabriel did the same.

The referee teleported, and in a split second, he was across the ring. He pointed to each of the boys in turn and called them to make ready. Each of them prepared themselves. His challenger took an offensive stance. Gabriel stood back in a more defensive formation.

In no time, the referee called for the match to begin. Michael stepped forward with a menacing demeanor. He looked almost nonchalant, as if he didn't take the fight seriously. Then, with a flash, he smirked at Gabriel and threw out his hand. Three jagged blocks of ice came rocketing toward Gabriel. Although startled, he was able to focus in time to block them with his telekinesis.

In the moment, Gabriel felt some pride in defending himself so adeptly. However, his pride was short-lived because before he noticed, Michael was on him and threw a shoulder-tackle into him. Michael's shoulder connected with Gabriel's sternum, and he immediately had the air knocked out of him. Gabriel slammed to the ground with a loud thud. When the world stopped spinning, he could hear the crowd *oohing*.

The announcer was just calling the hit a linebacker tackle as Gabriel stood up and found his footing. His ears were ringing from the blow. The world seemed wobbly, but regardless there was no time to wait for it to stop.

Moments later, the referee reset the two combatants to their starting positions. He moved Michael back to his side of the ring. When he made sure that the two were ready, he called for the fight to resume. Gabriel readied himself for Michael's imminent attack.

As expected, Michael once again threw several tattered shards of ice. However, this time Gabriel attempted to sidestep the wintery attack. He threw the closer shards aside with a push of telekinetic energy. Michael rushed in to close the distance. While Gabriel had been prepared for this attack, he wasn't prepared for Michael's schemes.

As Gabriel back peddled to avoid Michael's physical attack, he didn't see the icy puddle behind him. Just as Gabriel took a few steps, he noticed that his balance was compromised. He stumbled, then he slipped, and finally he dropped to the ground on his tailbone.

Another point for Michael.

Quickly, they reset their positions again. Gabriel was looking at Coach V, who was pointing to his head and motioning to forget it. Coach had told them this before. Sometimes having a short memory in a fight was the best thing you could have. Once you started dwelling on the problems, it was nearly impossible to come back.

Gabriel did bounce back to a degree. He scored a few points. The first was when Michael was rushing in for an attack, Gabriel swept his legs out from under him, scoring his first point. Michael, however, scored the next, followed by a second point for Gabriel.

Without much issue, Michael pulled ahead. He only needed one more point to win the match. Michael was fighting with a savage intensity. Gabriel took up a defensive front, refusing to concede any more easy points. To his credit, Gabriel was keeping the much more experienced Michael at a distance. This round had been going on for almost eight minutes when Jake approached the ring.

He was shocked to see Gabriel in the ring and his eyes narrowed. Moments later, his expression became confused and bewildered. An icy feeling flowed through his veins.

Inside the ring, Gabriel was constantly evading Michael's attacks. The whole crowd collectively gasped, which brought Jake's attention back to the fight. Up until that point, he had been looking down at the ground. His posture was shrunken. He looked up to see Gabriel evading attacks from his competitor.

Then Michael created a thick wall of ice and hid behind it. An opaque sheet blocked him from Gabriel's view. Gabriel hadn't seen anything like this before. *What kind of strategy is this? Is he hiding? Or is Michael trying to catch his breath?*

That must be it! Gabriel thought to himself. If he could rush Michael, he might be able to get a quick point. So, Gabriel rushed to the left side of the ice wall. However, Michael had other plans. As Gabriel was rushing to the left, he quickly came around the opposite side.

Meanwhile, the referee was attempting to follow Gabriel to keep him in his line of sight. He moved to the side of the ice wall that Gabriel had moved behind. But Michael wasn't there.

Just as Gabriel was moving around to the left, Michael made his move. He swung around the right side, keeping Gabriel in between himself and the referee. He immediately made his attack, striking Gabriel with a jagged knife-like icicle. The ice blade caught the padded uniform that Gabriel was wearing, which blocked most of it. However, the blade cut a small portion of the shirt, leaving a thin cut on his back.

Gabriel screamed in pain and dropped to the ground. In an instant, Michael made the ice dagger melt, hiding the attack from the referee and the crowd. The referee teleported back into the ring and immediately called the match.

"Michael wins!"

A few minutes later, Gabriel was rushed to the medic to make sure he wasn't too badly injured. When they got him to her room, the medic told them that the infused uniform did its job. It was nothing but a flesh wound. Simon and Coach weren't around. It was just Jin and Jake escorting him.

"I told you I was fine," Gabriel said to the group.

Jin walked with Gabriel back to their locker room. "Why don't you rest up? Your first loss is always a tough one."

"Yeah, thanks," Gabriel said, sounding defeated.

"Gabriel," Jin said, turning back to face him.

"Yeah?"

Jin made the same motion that Coach V used, the one that told him to forget. "Don't let this match define your career on the sparring team. Most combatants lose their first matches. Especially those who fight a senior with a winning record." Gabriel nodded.

Gabriel spent the next several minutes cleaning up from the match and getting a fresh uniform from the bag of extras. This one didn't have his number, but it would do.

After about fifteen minutes, both Simon and Coach V came rushing into the locker room.

"Good news, champ," said Simon.

"What?" Gabriel asked, more confused than anything.

"Coach V caught what Michael did."

"What do you mean?"

"That move at the end of the match, that was an illegal attack. Michael created an icicle dagger and attacked you with it. But no one else saw it. Everyone else thought he struck you with his hand."

Coach V had a tablet with him, and he turned it around to show Gabriel. On the screen was a recording of the fight from a higher vantage point. Coach V played the last few seconds of the fight. In the shot, when it was played back in super slow motion, he could see that Michael swung down with an ice knife in his hands. But in a second, it was gone.

Simon spoke up again. "Somehow Coach saw this, and he reported it to the officials. They took a look at the video recording. After making a vote, they disqualified Michael, which means you technically won the fight."

"Well, I don't know if we can say I won," Gabriel admitted. "But that means I move onto the next round, right?"

"Exactly," Simon said. "We should know your next opponent in just a few moments."

And with that, Simon and Coach V left the locker room. Gabriel felt renewed from the good news. A surge of excitement rushed through him, and he ran to get his gear back on. Just then he heard the door open behind him. He turned, expecting to see one of his teammates. However, it was someone else. An immediate twinge of panic stabbed his heart like a knife.

"It's good to see you, Gabriel."

Gabriel finally caught his breath. "It's good to see you too." He paused for a moment searching for the correct name. No, not name. The correct codename. "Duo, isn't it?"

Duo walked in with a smile on his face. "Yes, that's correct."

Duo's smile helped put Gabriel at ease, if only just a little. Gabriel had met Duo during the assault on Drake's underground lab. In fact, it was Duo who offered Gabriel the internship at the Guild because they had lost so many agents that day.

Duo approached Gabriel. His unkempt hair and wrinkled white lab coat looked the same as the last time Gabriel had seen him. He rubbed his hand through his hair and looked around the locker room.

"What brings you here?" Gabriel asked.

"What? A guy can't just be here to watch the sparring match?" Duo replied with a mock accusatory tone.

Gabriel gave him a look of disbelief.

"I have been keeping tabs on you since the incident last year. I just wanted to drop something off for you."

With that, Duo leaned forward and handed Gabriel a piece of fabric. Gabriel unfolded it and noticed it was his uniform. As soon as he realized what it was, Gabriel turned it over.

"It isn't ripped anymore," Gabriel said, running his hand along the place where the tear had been. "But it doesn't feel like it was sewn."

"That's my gift."

"You're an expert seamstress?"

"Ye...Er-uh, no, not exactly," Duo answered. "I'm an alchemist."

Gabriel paused for a moment but when he pieced it all together, he asked, "So, wait. You used your gift to fix my clothes?"

"Yes, fusing metal and fabric together is something of a specialty for me. I'm the one who made these particular uniforms, in fact. It was a favor that Coach V called in. I owed him one, so I made them. Top of the line. Better than anything mass-produced."

"That's amazing."

"Well, Gabriel, I do need to be going. I'll be leaving a pair of eyes to keep tabs on you," said Duo. Then he went to the door and pressed his hand against it.

There was an odd clicking sound like a latch was being undone and Duo opened the door. A younger man with thick messy black hair and grey eyes walked in. He had a shabby beard and a nonchalant expression.

"This is Agent Granite. He's a rather new agent, but he is experienced enough. I think you will be in very capable hands, Gabriel."

Agent Granite walked up in his suit, which Gabriel noticed was somewhat wrinkled. He held out a hand and shook Gabriel's. "Nice to meet you, Gabriel. I'm your shadow."

FILE #12

EYE OF THE STORM

After the agents left, Gabriel pulled the jersey over his head. He smoothed it out just as Simon came back into the room. "It looks like you will be competing in half an hour, Gabriel."

"Who's my opponent?" Gabriel asked as a bolt of shock plunged through him.

"It's a freshman with aerokinesis," Simon answered.

Gabriel nodded and then shot a stunned look over at Simon. "Wait, a freshman?"

"Yeah, not every school follows the same ideology as Coach V. There are plenty of schools that start their freshmen with little to no training. It can be a pretty controversial call on the coach's part. But sometimes it works out in their favor."

After Gabriel was ready, the two boys made their way to the arena for his match. By the time they got there, there was only a few minutes before the match. Coach V was there with a few substitutes on the bench.

The referee moved toward the gate and motioned for Gabriel to follow him. Gabriel did so and the referee closed the door behind him.

Inside, there was a young girl, who was noticeably short for her age. She might have reached to Gabriel's elbow. She had dirty blonde hair done in a short pixie cut, which added to her childlike appearance. Immediately, the referee went through the basic speech of conduct and fair competition. He strictly laid out what he would and wouldn't allow.

Gabriel held out a hand. "Best of luck!"

She smirked. "Go easy on me; it's my first match."

Afterwards, the referee shot backwards in a blur. Gabriel realized that he must have some enhanced speed type of gift.

When the referee called for the match to begin, Gabriel set into a defensive stand with his body ready to react to her first attack. However, she didn't move. Not even a muscle. Then out of nowhere, the most powerful gust of air pushed Gabriel over and he stumbled to the left. Then the air circled around and knocked him over to the right.

The referee called for a point for Katherine.

He reset and prepared himself. This time, she repeated her attack. A gust of wind pushed him around to the left. However, this time, Gabriel jumped up and allowed it to push him. He went sailing up in the air and then pushed himself using his telekinesis. He shot forward at Katherine like a rocket. When they collided, her diminutive size couldn't stand up to Gabriel, and she crashed down to the ground.

One point for Gabriel.

In the next round, she came back at him with another rush of air. This time it came right at him, but it was spinning as it collided with him. The gust was a small vortex that caused him to lose his footing. The blast of air hit him and pushed him back into the wall. He collided with the wall and slid to the ground.

One more point to Katherine.

She gained another point immediately by creating two gusts of wind. One hit Gabriel on his right shoulder, and the other hit his left leg. He flipped completely over and landed head over heels. However, he quickly corrected in the next round and received a point by pushing her with a similar force, knocking her over.

She countered in the next round with multiple bouts of wind directly at him, but then she knocked him down by pulling that wind toward herself. The vacuum effect pulled him toward her, making him lose his balance. She immediately took advantage of his loss of balance and slammed him backward to the ground.

One more point for Katherine.

While he regained his footing, Gabriel thought to himself, *I need to figure out a way to overcome her wind power.* "What can I do?" he muttered under his breath.

Just then, he saw Coach V motioning to him. He was pressing his hands together and miming a word that looked like "magnetic".

This time, a massive surge of air whipped straight at Gabriel and lifted him off the floor. He used his telekinesis to pull himself to the ground. Once his feet touched the ground, he focused as hard as he could on maintaining the connection.

Gabriel felt like a kite in a hurricane. He was being pushed and pulled by a small but concentrated surge of wind. It was everything he could do to not get caught up in the torrent.

When Katherine realized that Gabriel was somehow able to plant himself on the ground, she decided to ramp up her wind. She focused on Gabriel and caused a small tornado of air to begin spinning around the ring.

Almost impossibly, the wind began to move more and more forcefully. It was growing and growing in size, force, and deadliness. A look of shock covered her face for a moment. Without her controlling it, the wind began to start to fill the entire ring. Gabriel looked over to the referee. He was trying to run over to the exit, but, despite his superhuman speed, the wind caught him and he flew right to the top of the glass ceiling and collided with a terrible thud. Then he started spinning around the ring.

Gabriel's eyes widened. He knew that if he didn't get the referee down, he would continue to hit his head against the glass edges of the ceiling and…and…Gabriel didn't want to think about what that would mean.

So, instinctively Gabriel threw out a hand as he circled in the air. The referee froze in midair and Gabriel caught his hand, but the force of wind whipped him right out of his hand almost immediately. Instinctively, Gabriel caught him in the air, and he didn't move. He was held in place by his force of will.

After another few seconds, he pulled the referee toward himself. With a good deal of effort, he had the referee. His arms were burning, and his legs ached in protest. His body was begging him to stop, but he couldn't. Gabriel then looked at the girl, Katherine. He yelled at her to stop, but the wind swallowed up his words.

He tried again. "Katherine, cut it out! This is getting dangerous!"

By now, the officials outside of the ring realized things were not as they should be and started mobilizing. They rushed to the gate, but when they assessed the situation, they began to argue. Several moved to the doors, but two others argued that it would be too dangerous. A heated argument broke out as a result. But this was not a time to talk; this was a time to act.

Inside the ring, Gabriel continued to scream for Katherine to stop.

She tried yelling back several times, but the rush of wind made it hard to hear. Tears were welling up in her eyes. She yelled back with a twinge of panic in her voice. "I'm not doing this! I don't have control!"

Gabriel's eyes widened. She dropped to the ground and clutched her knees. Her eyes were filled with tears, and she was shuddering uncontrollably.

The uncontrollable winds raged around Gabriel. It was literally like being inside of a tornado. The wind twirled around him, forcing him to focus on his feet; otherwise, he would end up being caught in the whirlwind.

Gabriel looked back at the bench where his team was sitting. No one was sitting there anymore. He looked over at where the officials were standing by the gate. Coach V was among them, and it looked like he was giving the immobile officials a piece of his mind.

Well, it looked like no one was going to be helping him at the moment. So, Gabriel needed to do something. Options began running through his head. He could get the referee and himself to the gate and try and get out. He wasn't sure if that would work since the doors opened inward, and these intense winds might keep them from opening. But he needed to get the girl to stop the cyclone.

Gabriel looked back to Katherine. She was still on the ground, holding her knees to her chest. Gabriel knew what he needed to do. He gripped the referee under his arm and heaved himself in the direction of Katherine. He was able to shield them from the force of the winds, but it was exerting all of his energy. As he neared her, he noticed it was harder to hold the referee. Not only were his arms quickly losing strength, but the sheer amount of sweat he was exuding was making it hard to keep a grip.

After a few minutes, he made it to her. With his one hand on the referee, he knelt down to her. Although he was inches away from her, he had to yell to be heard over the torrent of wind.

"Katherine, you have to get it together! You have to stop this!"

"I'm not doing this! I started the winds, but they aren't under my control anymore. This isn't me!" she yelled back, tears in her eyes.

He put an arm on her shoulder. "Katherine, what is your gift?"

She sniffed loudly. "I can control wind."

"So, you can use that gift to stop this, can't you?" he asked.

"I don't think I can. It's too strong now."

"I don't believe that!" he protested.

She looked at him as if she was offended. Then she studied his eyes. There was something there. Not accusation or anger. Something like hope.

"If you don't believe in yourself, who will?" he asked. "You are clearly the strongest person in this ring. I know that, and the whole crowd knows that. There's no way you won't win this whole meet."

"Get out of here," she said with a smirk. "I'm a freshman."

"Probably the strongest freshman ever," he said with a smile.

"But how?" Her voice quivered.

"I can't do it for you, Katherine. You have all of the power inside of you. But you have to pick yourself up, dust yourself off, and try. That's the only way things will get better."

She looked around the ring. The winds were whipping around like a hurricane. Her hands trembled. Gabriel looked at her, willing her to believe in herself.

After a few seconds, she nodded in agreement. Then she stood, and her eyes glowed. He hadn't noticed it before, but they turned an almost imperceptible shade of blue. Almost white in appearance. She held her hands to her side, and Gabriel could tell that she was willing the winds to stop.

At first, nothing happened. Beads of sweat covered her forehead. The strain of it was clear on her face. Gabriel could see that she was using the last bit of her strength. He whispered, "You got this. Come on, Katherine."

She started to move her hands in the opposite direction of the cyclone. Then she shot out a burst of wind that smashed against the vortex. Almost immediately, the winds died down to an imperceptible breeze.

She turned to Gabriel, but he was out cold on the floor.

***

Gabriel's eyes shot open. A small huddled group of people was around him. It took a second for his eyes to focus and make sense of who was around him. It was Coach V, Jake, Simon, and several other members of the team.

"How you feeling, champ?" asked Coach V.

With more effort than it should have taken, he leaned up. He smiled and let out one short laugh. "Champ. That's funny."

"You don't need to win to be a champ, Gabriel. You did good in there."

He tried to sit up, but a campus medic asked him to wait a few more minutes before getting up. She checked his vital signs again, just to be sure he was not suffering from a concussion or any other injuries. When he was cleared, he stood and joined his team.

He spent the next hour showering and then being attended to by the team physician. Simon spoke with him after on behalf of Coach V.

"You did the right thing in there, Gabriel."

"I hope so," he answered, looking up at the television in the locker room. It was a college sports cast, recapping the events of the day.

"Gabriel, listen," said Simon, pausing. "I know winning is important to you. But that was really cool of you."

"What? Passing out in front of a stadium?"

Simon smiled and laughed. "No, I don't know what you said to her, but that was pretty cool. Helping her out like that. I think Coach was right to put his faith in you."

He stood up and moved toward the door. "Check out this broadcast. I think you will like it."

In a flash, the television changed to another station. There were two people on the screen, one of which was Simon. The other was a female news anchor. She was speaking to the camera and telling the viewers about what just happened. Then it cut to a short scene of the event. It was odd seeing it from the outside.

Then it cut back to the two of them, and the news anchor was introducing Simon and asking him, "So, tells us a little bit of what you saw."

"Well, you have to know Gabriel to understand what happened. He is the kind of dude that doesn't leave anyone behind. He's a good friend and a brother."

Gabriel looked at Simon with a smirk. Simon smiled back. "I meant it, man."

Then Simon pushed the door open and left.

***

That evening, the awards were given out. Gabriel's team came in second based on points, but it was a close second. Then they announced that Katherine's school had won. They erupted into applause and cheers when it was announced. Lucien threw Gabriel a dirty look. Simon moved over to where Gabriel was standing.

"Don't worry about him," he said. "He's upset that you lost your fight."

"No kidding," Gabriel said, wrapping his arms around his chest.

"He's been blaming you for the loss. He said if you had scored a few more hits, we could have won."

"Great," Gabriel said. "Insult to injury."

Just then, Gabriel noticed Katherine on the stage. She took the microphone from the podium. "I wanted to say something really quick. Is that okay?"

Her team went silent. The crowd followed suit and stopped clapping and cheering.

Katherine spoke up, her small voice aided by the microphone. "I wanted to thank a very special person for this victory. Yes, my team, our coaches, the staff, and all of them. But this is to a person not on our team. Someone who did the right thing, the hard thing. I wanted to thank Gabriel Green for helping me in that ring. This victory feels good, but the victory

I feel inside thanks to you is so much more important. So, thank you!"

Gabriel looked back at Lucien with a smile stretching from ear to ear. He made eye contact with Lucien and raised his eyebrows. *What do you think of that?* he thought.

Lucien rolled his eyes in reply and walked off.

Coach V put his massive hand on Gabriel's shoulder. "Nice job, son. You did good."

FILE #13

THE CHEATER

Gabriel was given special privilege on Monday to miss classes. An honor that he took full advantage of. He slept in, rested, and skipped practice. Jake was thoroughly annoyed at this, mumbling under his breath when he left that morning. He assumed Jake was just jealous that he didn't have to go to classes.

On Tuesday, he went to class like usual. The day started off relatively normal. However, Gabriel noted that as he moved around campus people began noticing him more. He wasn't sure why, but he was getting odd looks and shifting glances. As he passed through crowds, people stopped talking in their normal tones and began using hushed whispers.

He wondered if it was because of the meet. People were probably upset that he ended up losing his match. Lucien was undoubtedly spreading rumors about him. *Fun times*, he thought to himself. He did his best not to dwell on it as he trudged on and tried not to think about what people were saying about him behind his back.

When he got into class that morning, a student nearby him asked him if he could sign his newspaper. Gabriel gave him an odd look, but when the young man handed Gabriel his newspaper, he understood why. The campus newspaper had a picture from the meet with Gabriel on the front page. It was a picture of Gabriel exiting the final match. Admittedly, he looked horrible. His eyes were twitching and his expression was completely dazed.

But even still, he was on the newspaper, and front page nonetheless. Next, his eyes found the headline. "Substitute Saves Competitor". Gabriel scanned the article. It told the circumstances of how Gabriel was brought in to substitute that day and elaborated on the first match. The writer embellished many of the details, making it sound like Michael was some kind of villain. Next, it went on to detail the fight with Katherine. Once again, the situation was not nearly as perilous as the author made it sound. According to the article, Gabriel was a knight in shining armor, and Katherine was a damsel in distress.

Gabriel rolled his eyes at that. He didn't really even save her. He had just convinced her that she could stop the whirlwind herself. So, Gabriel scribbled a signature. "Hey, don't believe everything you read, okay? It wasn't nearly that exciting." Then he handed the paper back to the student and prepared for class.

***

The next day, Gabriel went to practice after his classes. It was a pretty routine week, despite the irregular amount of attention Gabriel was receiving.

The following evening, Gabriel planned on meeting up with Serena, Simon, and Jake. It was too long since they had all gotten to hang out. Gabriel noticed that this semester it became harder to coordinate with everyone's schedules. However, that evening everyone agreed to meet for pizza at Big Chicago's.

Big Chicago's was a fantastic pizza place on campus where the group usually hung out. It had the best pizza in the area. It was always packed, so getting a seat was sometimes a chore.

However, Gabriel got there early, and Simon ordered their usual.

Serena arrived shortly after. The three of them sat at the table and shared stories about the semester so far. Serena was working for the campus newspaper, *The Vision*. She enjoyed writing, and she thought that it would be a good way to expand her writing abilities. Mostly she focused on songwriting, but this was something she had decided she was going to do at the end of last semester.

Simon, on the other hand, was now working with Coach V as the sparring team's assistant manager. He was telling Serena about some of the job when Gabriel interrupted and told her that Simon was perfect for the job. His gift of technopathy made him invaluable to the team. Gabriel told her about how Simon was able to bring up footage of the meet on Saturday that proved Michael had cheated. Without that footage, Gabriel probably would not have moved on to the next match.

Serena then asked Gabriel how he liked being on the sparring team. Gabriel got somewhat shy, as he didn't always like the idea of being the center of attention. But with his friends, he knew he could be completely honest.

"It's a ton of work. Coach V works us to the bone. But I love working with Simon, Coach V, and Jake."

Simon interrupted. "That reminds me, where's Jake?"

Gabriel and Serena both looked around the room. There was still no sign of him. They had been there for over half an hour, but he hadn't show up.

"Now that I think about it, I haven't seen him much at practice," Simon added.

"Really?" asked Gabriel.

"Yeah, he hasn't been coming as often as he usually does."

Just as Gabriel was looking at Simon, he noticed Jake come into Big Chicago's. Gabriel waved Jake over. However, Jake turned and walked to the front. He seemed to be ordering food.

Gabriel told the group that he would go get him.

As he walked over to Jake, he felt a twinge of worry. Jake looked odd. When he approached, Gabriel put his arm on Jake's shoulder. "Hey, we are over here," he started.

Jake recoiled.

"What's the matter?" Gabriel asked.

"Nothing, I...uh, just have a lot of work to do," answered Jake. Jake grabbed his food and started to walk away. Gabriel followed him.

"Hey, what practice are you going to tomorrow?" Gabriel asked.

"I—I don't know."

"Well, why don't we go to the afternoon one, and we can get in a little sparring time. I want to see how much better you've gotten with that fire attack."

"Uh, I don't think I will be able to make that one."

"Ok, how about next week?"

"I don't know. My schedule is kind of crazy right now."

Gabriel didn't understand because they had an almost identical schedule.

"What about this weekend?" Gabriel asked. "Do you want to hang out and do something?"

Jake turned around and looked Gabriel dead in the eyes. "Dude, take a hint. I'm busy." Then Jake pushed past Gabriel and continued walking into the night. Gabriel stood there for several minutes in utter shock. Several people walked past, staring at him awkwardly. Although they made comments about him, he didn't respond. He didn't even move. He couldn't understand what had just happened.

***

On Friday, Gabriel went to the afternoon practice. He usually attended these practices, because he liked to get his classes finished in the morning whenever possible. He and Claudio were stretching in the corner. Several other teammates were working out or sparring on the mats around the workout room.

Eames was on a bench with his crutches next to him. He was healing quickly, but he would be out for a few weeks at the least. The assistant coach was working with him on some physical therapy stretches to help him heal.

Meanwhile, Gabriel was wrapped up in what was happening on the news. He was in the workout room, running on a treadmill, when the breaking news came across the screen. One of the most famous agencies was on the news. The Cobalt Core, an agency based in Germania, was reporting on their most recent mission's success.

A man with golden blond hair was on the screen. His handsome features were highlighted by the camera, and he was eating up every minute of it. He had dark emerald eyes, sharp facial features, and a dazzling smile. Gabriel recognized him before his name even came across the screen. Lionheart, head of the Cobalt Corp, smiled into the camera.

Agents of the Corp called themselves "knights," and their clothing matched it. Like all of the knights, he was wearing a long coat with regalia along the edges and gold buttons down the middle. His shirt was bright white with ruffles. When he finished his introductions, the reporter asked him about the mission.

Lionheart was a very confident commander, but not exactly cocky. His agency was one of the most well-known. Not because of marketing or public relation stunts, but because they were quite possibly the biggest and most well-funded agency in the world. The Kingdom of Germania directly funded the agency to make sure they were receiving top-of-the-line equipment and materials.

Gabriel looked away as the reporter ended the news piece. Unfortunately for Gabriel, the reporter didn't ask anything of much detail. Just generic questions about whether the mission was a success or not. Either way, he was disappointed.

Agencies were of a special interest to Gabriel, especially recently. Like many other young people, Gabriel looked up to agents like Lionheart because they protected the world.

There was a loud clink that broke his reverie. Gabriel noticed Derek lifting weights with a single arm. Gabriel couldn't even lift that much weight with both hands and someone else's help. Gabriel shook his head and called out, "Need a hand there, Derek?" he asked in a joking tone.

Derek looked over at him and smiled that huge toothy grin. When he smiled like that, he looked like the Cheshire Cat. Then he continued his reps. Gabriel shook his head and stepped off of the treadmill. He decided that was enough running for one day. Especially if he wasn't being forced to run.

Just then, Lucien came storming through the hall. He kicked a medicine ball across the room, grabbed his duffle bag and stormed back out of the room, punching the wall as he exited. Everyone's eyes were as wide as saucers. Gabriel looked at Claudio. "What was that about?"

"I have no idea," Claudio replied.

Claudio and Gabriel looked over at Eames, who was laying on his back. He was watching everything upside down. Gabriel smirked at his confused expression. "What am I seeing?" he asked, squinting.

A few seconds later, Coach V walked in with Simon and Jin. He looked around the room. Noticing the tension in the air, Coach V waved a hand in the air. "So, you all saw that, hmm?" he asked. When everyone collectively nodded their heads, Coach V groaned. "Well, I'm sure you're wondering what happened."

There was a pause, as if Coach V was expecting an answer. However, no one said anything.

"It'll be no surprise to you when I say that Lucien has become increasingly volatile. His attitude has degraded this year to an almost intolerable level. He's berated team members, refused to partner with those he felt were weak, and overall treated the staff with something less than respect. Now,

I have overlooked some of these behaviors, and others have only recently been brought to my attention. I apologize for both of these."

The whole team stood in complete shock.

"Maybe I overlooked those things because he was a great competitor, or maybe it was because I didn't want to notice them. Maybe I made excuses because I wanted to win too much. However, something came up this week, and it could not be ignored."

"What's that, Coach?" asked Claudio.

Coach V paused for a moment. He looked around the room, and Gabriel could have sworn that he looked more upset than he had ever seen him before.

"Someone brought it to my attention that Lucien was cheating. We examined the evidence. It was rather overwhelming evidence, and it could not be allowed to continue. So, we brought the evidence to Lucien and asked him if he wanted to admit to it."

Coach V looked at Simon and then at Jin.

"What do you mean, 'he was cheating' Coach?" asked Derek.

"It was brought to my attention that Lucien was using magnetic bands on his wrists. These bands were worn on both wrists and they offered him some enhanced electric capabilities. Now, I am sure all of you know the use of any power-augmenting gear is prohibited."

"What did Lucien say?" asked Avery.

Coach V looked at the ground and then back up at the crowd. "He did not take it well, as you can all see."

"So, what does this mean for the team?" asked Eames.

"Well, we will continue as usual. We will be changing the order of rank of captain, for one thing. Would everyone please join me in a round of applause in appointing Jin Kenichi the position of team captain."

Everyone clapped in unison. Jin didn't even flinch. She stood stoically, not smiling or even nodding in appreciation. Jin held up a hand to stop everyone. When the room silenced, she said, "Thank you," and that was all.

Coach V smirked seriously. It was one of the oddest things Gabriel noticed about Coach. He could look completely serious even when he smiled. Next, Coach spent the next several minutes going over some of the upcoming dates for the sparring team. He informed the team when their next meet would be in three weeks.

After Coach V finished, Claudio grabbed Gabriel. "All right, string bean, let's go spar."

"Awesome," answered Gabriel. He wiped his face with his towel and followed him.

"Yeah, I need to make sure you don't get too cocky after your 'heroic weekend' saving everyone," Claudio said jokingly, making air quotes with his fingers.

Gabriel rolled his eyes. "You know me, man. I am about to snatch that open starters spot."

A shadowed figure, unseen by the team, was just sitting up as Gabriel and Claudio passed by. He was working out in the corner quietly. Gabriel didn't realize it, but the figure stood up after hearing what he said. He grabbed his towel from around his neck and look at him with something like fire in his eyes.

Just then, Derek walked past. "Oh, hey," he said to the figure. "I didn't realize you were at practice today, Jake."

Jake sneered and walked off to the locker rooms.

FILE #14

A TALE OF TWO AGENTS

After practice, Coach V invited Gabriel down to his office. Gabriel sat in front of Coach V's desk. Coach V had a serious look on his face. Unsure of what to say or do, Gabriel sat in silence. The silence lasted for several moments.

Finally, Coach V stood up. He looked at Gabriel and held out a tablet. "Gabriel, I asked you down here to talk about your role in our organization."

"All right," Gabriel answered, looking as serious as Coach.

"You know that agents are very popular. Many of them rise to the same celebrity status that actors and athletes achieve. Many are household names because of the cases they have solved and the recognition they have acquired."

Gabriel nodded.

"It's a lot of pressure being an agent. The testing alone is grueling. Then you add all of the requirements, the emotional stress, and the physical danger. It's a big job."

Gabriel wasn't sure if Coach V was trying to persuade him to quit or encourage him in some roundabout way, but he listened nonetheless.

Coach sighed. "There are two types of agents, Gabriel." Coach V put his tablet on the desk and tapped it a few times. The television screen behind him lit up with the face of a woman. Underneath her, there was a field of text. The woman had olive skin and short auburn hair. Her eyes were a pale grey, not unlike Gabriel's. The picture of the woman changed from a front view to a profile shot, and then it cycled through every few seconds. Beside the picture the text began scrolling with information.

"Who...who's she?" asked Gabriel. "She looks kind of familiar."

Just as Coach V was about to answer, a word popped out to Gabriel.

"Wait, she's telekinetic?" asked Gabriel. "So, is she an agent too?"

"Yes, well she *was* at least," answered Coach V. "I can't tell you her name, but her handle was Agent Mal."

There was a long pause. At first Gabriel wasn't sure what he meant. But he quickly understood what that very specific tone meant. Gabriel wasn't sure what to say at first. Finally, he gained the courage to ask, "What happened to her?"

Coach V paused for several seconds. His eyes scanned his desk, not looking at Gabriel. Then Coach ran a hand along his thick, dark arms and cleared his throat. "The other agent was Agent Gamut." He clicked a button on his tablet, and the picture on the screen changed to a man with curly blond hair and piercing blue eyes. He had a shine to his eyes and a megawatt smile.

Gabriel thought for a while. He racked his brain, trying to remember if he ever heard of this agent. He looked like he was an important person, but Gabriel didn't think he knew him.

"Like I said, many agents become celebrities. Some get endorsement deals for sports drinks or health insurance. Others go on to become movie stars, news anchors, or reality TV stars. Agent Gamut was positive that this was his destiny. He was sure he would become a celebrity. He was a very skilled agent.

He had all of the power you would want an agent to have, however he was cocky and stubborn."

"What was his gift?" asked Gabriel.

"He had an adaptive ability where his skin could change to different a consistency if he needed. It was a very unique and useful ability." With that, Coach paused again. He pulled off his hat and rubbed his short salt-and-pepper hair. Gabriel couldn't tell if Coach was more frustrated or sad. Emotions and thoughts were clearly swirling around in his mind, that much was certain. But exactly what he was feeling was a mystery.

"So, what happened to him?" Gabriel asked, a quiver in his voice.

Coach V turned in his chair and faced the screen. Now both faces were showing up side by side. "I can't give you all of the details, all right? But several years ago, our agency got intelligence that there was a group working on a plan that…" He trailed off for a moment as if he was searching for the words. "Well, let's just say that it would have been a devastating situation."

He paused to take a sip of water. Gabriel sat in silence, completely engrossed in the story. Although it took mere moments, to Gabriel, it seemed like an eternity. Finally, Coach V continued.

"When we made our move to stop them, Agent Gamut and Agent Mal were both there. Agent Gamut was supposed to wait in position, but he wasn't following orders. He was thinking with his ego and emotions, not his head."

Gabriel was almost afraid to ask, but his curiosity compelled him. "What happened next?"

"Agent Mal was on the scene. She was the tank in this mission. So, she was at the front line, playing defense for us. Agent Gamut was supposed to be the rogue, so it was his job to sneak into a position and remain there so we could get someone behind the enemy. So, Mal and her team got their orders when everyone was ready and moved up. But Gamut jumped the gun, and she heard over her earpiece that Gamut wasn't following orders. She and her team were at the door, ready to move in."

"She rushed in and saved the day, right?" said Gabriel.

"Not exactly son. Missions aren't like you read in comic books or see in movies. Sometimes it isn't that easy."

Gabriel's face fell.

"So, the team was ready to move in, and Mal got us, I mean…them inside. The team surrounded the suspects. However, Gamut was caught."

"What an idio—" Gabriel cut himself off, although his fists were clenched and he was biting his lip.

"The suspects tried to use the captured agent as a bargaining chip. They said if they were let go, they would return him. The commanding officer told the team to stand down and not to play ball with the suspects. However, Mal had other ideas."

On the edge of his seat, Gabriel looked at Coach with wide-eyed anticipation.

"The suspects probably had no intention of releasing Gamut, and when the situation went sideways, they threatened to kill him. Agent Mal tried to save him, and she disobeyed her orders to do so. Unfortunately, it was too late. She couldn't save him. But she didn't give up the mission. Even when it seemed the suspects were about to get away, she sacrificed herself to stop them."

"What do you mean, 'she sacrificed herself'?" asked Gabriel.

"Mal had a special skill that she called her ultimate move. She moved to the suspects and used her telekinetic gift to create what she called a 'tele-stasis field'. It was a concentrated field of telekinetic energy that trapped anything inside of it permanently."

Gabriel's jaw dropped, sitting there in complete astonishment.

"Unfortunately, she centered the field around herself, and she was trapped in the field as well. It trapped the suspects, and we were able to detain the rest. Even though the mission was a success on paper, it was one of the worst missions of my career."

"So, you *were* there," Gabriel said.

With a sigh, Coach answered, "Yes, I was. I was the commanding officer there. It was one of the first ops where I was the lead. I lost two agents that day, and I relegated myself to operations recruiter instead of field leader."

"Why?"

"Well, even though it was a success, I lost two agents. Both Mal and Gamut were trapped in that tele-stasis field. Those were losses that were on my shoulders. So, I resigned from field duty."

"But Coach, you couldn't know that Gamut would do that. That wasn't your fault."

"I didn't know he would, but I knew him pretty well. I should have foreseen that and chosen a more fitting agent. It could have saved two lives."

"Coach V, it wasn't your fault."

"Gabriel, I didn't tell you that story to debate the rights and wrongs of my leadership skills."

"So, why did you?'

"Well, why do you think?" asked Coach.

"I guess to understand that you have to follow orders."

Coach V shook his head. "No, actually that's not it at all."

Gabriel looked at him with a furrowed brow and scratched his ear.

Coach V smirked. "It wasn't because they both disobeyed an order. But why they did it that defined them. Think about it. What do you think Gamut's reasons were?" As he said that, he put out his left hand.

"Well, based on what you told me, I'm guessing he thought he could get the drop of the suspects and get all the glory."

"Exactly. He saw an opening, and he assumed he could spring in there to stop the enemies. I tried to get him to keep his position, but he said he had a perfect opportunity to get them all together. I told him not to move, but he was convinced he could get them all by himself."

"Wow. And that's how he got himself caught."

"Indeed. He didn't realize there was a second group coming up behind him. He was surrounded before he could do anything."

Gabriel let that hit him. Because of one reckless action, both of those agents were captured.

Coach V held out his right hand. "What about Mal?"

"I don't know" said Gabriel.

"I think Mal knew the cost, but she knew she had a chance to make things right. Agent Mal put her allies and the safety of the public before herself. She made the ultimate decision to protect and serve."

The weight of the words filled the room. Gabriel sat in silence, letting those words soak into his being.

"This woman was something of your predecessor. She was one of the best agents we had back then. She worked well in a team, and she wasn't a glory hog. And back then, agencies weren't as well-respected as they are today."

Gabriel nodded. In his history classes, he'd learned that early on, countries didn't trust the agencies. They were an unknown investment early on. But once they proved how useful they could be, the world took notice.

"Mal was an extremely skilled gifted. She helped us more than we could ever have dreamed."

"And you want me to fill her shoes?" asked Gabriel.

Coach smirked, but it was so brief it was almost unnoticeable. "Not exactly. But maybe one day, you can rise to her level."

He paused for a second.

"You see, Mal sacrificed herself. She believed that despite her power, she was just a woman. She believed that the mission came before anyone else. So, she made the ultimate sacrifice."

Gabriel was leaning in, completely unaware that he was doing so. His eyes were wide with anticipation. "Are they still down in the sewers?"

"No, no they aren't," answered Coach V. "Shortly afterwards, a backup team got to the scene and we were able to retrieve them."

"And what about the tele-stasis field? Were you able to get through it?"

"No, it is still active with everyone still frozen inside."

Gabriel looked at Coach V in shock. He didn't understand. He stuttered for a few seconds without the ability to utter a single world. *How in the world could someone maintain that much telekinetic energy to keep an orb of it active for that long?* Gabriel wondered. He didn't understand it, but part of him hoped he could find out someday.

"This brings me to why I asked you to come down here today, Gabriel." Coach V paused for a second as he came back to his desk and sat down. "You and Mal shared one of the most immensely powerful gifts that we have discovered. As you can see from the example I just explained."

Gabriel nodded in agreement. He had never heard of such a feat. Maintaining a field of pure telekinetic energy and trapping multiple people inside of it. Gabriel couldn't believe it. He was still trying to piece together how it was even possible.

"When we first talked about you becoming a part of the organization, this is what I was referring to when I said not everyone makes it back."

Gabriel nodded.

Coach V continued without an answer. "This is what it's like being an agent. Some get in for the right reasons, and others just want the fame, money, and the glory. However, I still have one question for you, Gabriel."

"What is it?" Gabriel asked.

"Which type of agent will you be?" Coach V asked, his tone completely sincere.

Gabriel sat in silence for a few moments. Then he opened his mouth but quickly closed it when he thought better of it. He waited a few more seconds.

"Coach," Gabriel said, pausing to swallow. "I want to be like Agent Mal, but…"

He paused again for a few moments. His throat felt like it had a lump in it. He swallowed and felt like he could breathe again.

"But what?" asked Coach V.

Gabriel breathed deeply. "Part of me wonders if I have what it takes to be that brave."

"Everyone thinks that bravery is something that you have all of the time. It isn't necessarily something you can learn or practice. When the moment comes, you have to make that choice. No one knows how they will react in a life or death situation. But based on what I heard about your last semester, I think you are a brave person."

Gabriel nodded in agreement. "Thanks, Coach."

"So, speaking of making the right call, I have your next assignment."

FILE #15

MIND GAMES

The following afternoon in class, Gabriel was listening to Professor Pius' lecture. From his seat in the back, he could look down on the whole classroom. The professor was continuing a lecture from the other day, focusing on the rights and wrongs as they concerned the gifted.

"Should the gifted be allowed to use their power to do whatever they want?"

A hand rose quickly in reply. He called on a student, a girl from the sparring team named Zoey. This week, she had a stripe of blue in her hair. "Definitely not. The gifted have a responsibility.

"A wonderful point."

Another hand rose up. The boy who rose his hand was not a gifted, but he said, "Well, the gifted have powers unlike anything in ancient history. Can we really hold them to the same rules of right and wrong?"

Pius raised his hands in a questioning gesture. "Well said, Mr. Masons."

A third hand rose up. "The student that is right is always the same, regardless of when, where, and why."

Gabriel found himself nodding. He wanted to raise his hand and add to that, but he felt a tinge of worry in doing so.

Pius continued the debate on what was right and wrong. Gabriel noticed a pattern as the lecture went on. Each time a point was made by a student, he would turn and play devil's advocate. He would present whoever spoke with a counter argument. He would even counter points he made earlier in the discussion. Regardless of the point, he always seemed to offer a contrary argument.

Maybe that's just part of the class, Gabriel thought to himself.

Professor Pius ended the class with one final thought. "What do you think would happen if the gifted were the ones on top of the world? If the gifted were the ones who ruled the planet?"

Gabriel looked down and noticed Jake in the front rows. He must have missed when Jake started taking this class. He'd never seen him in class before. Jake was really engaged as the professor spoke. Normally, Jake was the student in the backrow, snoring. Regardless, it was good to see Jake taking an interest in a class.

"Think on that tonight, and I want everyone to come back next class with a one-page arguing whether you are for or against this idea."

With a flourish, Pius turned around and began to collect his belongings from the desk and putting them into his handcrafted leather suitcase.

As the classroom was quickly emptying, Gabriel hung back, taking his time packing his bag. He looked down at Pius out of the corner of his eye, but noticed a figure walking down toward the professor. He looked closer and realized it was Jake. Whatever they were discussing, Jake looked like he was agreeing.

Just then, Gabriel's attention was taken when a group of students walked by the door. Zoey called out to catch up with them. The crowd stopped which caused one of the people to notice Gabriel.

"Hey, man," said Derek. He moved in and gave Gabriel an elaborate high five that Gabriel had a hard time keeping up with. They clasped hands, knocked their elbows together, followed by two fist bumps, and ending with a flurry of high fives and fist bumps with both hands.

Eames moved awkwardly toward Zoey. With his medical boot on, Eames wasn't able to move as quickly as he normally could. Which, for a speedster like him, was a difficult adjustment. His poor coordination was on full display. He stood awkwardly next to Zoey, leaving Gabriel to wonder if they were seeing each other now.

As if hearing Gabriel's thought, Eames said, "Gabriel, I didn't know you and Zoey met last semester. She was telling me last night on our date."

"Yeah, we met during our placement test."

"That's right," she said, making a face at Eames for his awkward statement.

Gabriel was pretty sure he was just trying to brag that he had a girlfriend now. But thankfully Derek changed the conversation before it got too weird.

"How are you doing after the meet?" asked Derek.

"I'm pretty good man. I've been sorer than I ever have in my life though. Who would have thought that a tornado would do that?" Gabriel said jokingly.

The group laughed. Eames even punched Gabriel in the arm, calling him a big shot. Although it wasn't intentionally hard, Gabriel winced. Awkwardly, he tried to cover it up by faking a cough and raising his fist to block his mouth. For the most part, the soreness was bearable. But when someone hit him, even playfully, it really hurt.

Gabriel tried his best to keep an eye on what was going on with Pius and Jake as the group kept talking. He was too wrapped up in what Pius was saying to pay much attention. When the group laughed, Gabriel forced a fake laugh, attempting to blend into the conversation. Although he knew it sounded fake, he kept one eye on Pius and Jake. A fleeting thought passed his mind about how agents kept their cool in these situations.

As he heard someone make a mocking comment about another professor, Gabriel saw them shake hands down by Pius' desk. Jake looked like he was thanking him for something. Then Jake turned and started walking up the stairs past them. Gabriel turned his attention back to the group. Someone was saying something about hanging out, but he missed where. Jake saw the group and stepped to the other side of the stairs, his eyes narrowed on Gabriel.

"So, you have to come hang out with us?" Derek was asking Gabriel.

Jake was moving past the group in earshot of the invitation. Gabriel noticed him pause for a moment as he passed by them. Derek noticed Jake as he did so. Jake kept on walking, too proud to join the group. As much as he wanted to ask, he couldn't. No, he wouldn't ask.

"So, what do you think?" asked Eames.

Gabriel wasn't looking at them. He was looking at Jake. Just then, Gabriel tried to call out to Jake, but something caught in his throat. Was it his own pride? Maybe his fear of rejection again. Jake was moving through the doorway and he rounded the corner out of sight.

Gabriel's attention came back to the group. He thought for a moment and looked back at the doorway. Should he go after his friend, or should he get back to the task—no, the mission—at hand? He looked down at Pius. The professor was starting to lock up his brown leather suitcase. What should he do?

Gabriel took a step up the stairs toward Jake. But then he thought better of it. Time was of the essence. He stopped himself. He turned around and started walking down toward Professor Pius.

Then he realized that the group was still standing there, looking at him. He turned to them. "I'm sorry guys. I need to talk to Pius about an assignment. I'll catch up with you later."

They all looked at him oddly. Gabriel could hear Zoey ask if he was always so scattered. He cringed but didn't hear Eames reply.

Then he asked Pius, who was walking away at this point, if he could speak with him. Pius turned around and looked at Gabriel. The light sent a glare over his small spectacles, so he couldn't see Pius' eyes. Pius smirked and looked at his watch.

"Office hours are in about half an hour. Why don't you come on up to my office then?"

"Thank you so much, sir."

"Do you know where it is?"

Gabriel nodded.

***

Half an hour later, Gabriel found his way up to the faculty offices. It was a tall building where all of the professors and staff members had their offices. Well, most of the staff. Some teachers, like Coach V, kept their offices where they taught. Gabriel recalled overhearing Coach talk about how he enjoyed the seclusion that his office provided, since most of the other professors were in the noticeably busy tower.

Without too much difficulty, Gabriel found the correct hallway. Although there were numerous markings on which offices were which, the numbering system didn't make much sense to Gabriel. However, he finally made it to Pius's office. Gabriel knocked and when Pius answered, he entered.

Pius was sitting at his desk, a massive mahogany piece that dominated the room. The room had some posters on the walls. He noticed a poster of a championship winning soccer team in Spain. Gabriel was quite certain that Pius hailed from Spain. At that moment, Gabriel found himself kind of liking Pius a little bit more because of his own love of soccer.

Pius stood and straightened his shirt and vest. His coat was hanging near Gabriel on a coatrack. He motioned for Gabriel to take a seat in the chair in front of his desk. Gabriel slid into the dark mahogany chair that matched the desk. He sat his book bag down at his feet.

When Gabriel looked up, he scanned Pius' desk. There were several unique pieces on the desk. The first was a black statue of a sphinx on the right corner. The other was a golden bust of what Gabriel could only assume was an Egyptian pharaoh.

"Have you spent a lot of time in Egypt?" Gabriel asked.

"Some, yes. The culture fascinates me. Are you familiar with their mythology?" Pius asked.

"Not extensively. I mean we learned about them in fourth or fifth grade, I think."

"Did you know in Egyptian mythology, the gods created the world out of the primordial chaos? The gods, Ra and Horus, Osiris, and Isis created the entire universe from the chaotic energy. But then, there was this battle between chaos and order when the god, Set, moved to disrupt their order. It is all quite fascinating."

"Really? So, it sounds like chaos and order are a big part of the Egyptian culture."

"Indeed, they are. Very important. It played into their ideals on kingship, work, and religion," answered Pius folding his hands together.

Gabriel paused for a moment. "So, which do you see yourself aligning with?"

Pius sat back for a moment and looked up at the ceiling. "That's such an intriguing question. Don't we all have both sides in ourselves? Order and chaos battle for supremacy every single day in our hearts."

Pius was a master at dodging questions, and his smooth delivery was second to none. He looked around the room and made an all-encompassing gesture. "We are but pieces in this mess of chaos and order, are we not? So, I notice you eyeing my championship poster over there. Are you a soccer fan?"

"Yes, very much so. I played back in high school."

"Wonderful. What position?"

"I started on defense, but I played some midfield too."

"Ah, a very difficult position indeed. Both of them. You must have been very talented to be so versatile."

"I was all right."

Pius smiled. "Nonsense. Midfield in soccer is one of the most difficult and demanding positions in all of athletics. Not only do you have to play both offense and defense, but you are often in charge of the transition from one to the other. Don't be so modest, Gabriel."

Gabriel looked down and his face became a subtle shade of red.

"Speaking of which. I heard about your heroics at the sparring team meet. What a strange turn of events."

"Yeah." Gabriel paused, trying to determine which part he was referring to. "It was such a wild day."

"What was it like being in that tornado?" Pius asked, sitting forward in his chair. "That must have been absolutely terrifying."

"It was really terrifying. But I am glad that everyone made it out in one piece." Gabriel began to relax. He sat back in his chair and let down his guard.

Pius began congratulating Gabriel on his performance. Even though he lost, Pius said that Gabriel's demeanor in the ring was nothing short of heroic.

For several minutes, Pius buttered Gabriel up until he had completely let his guard down. Pius sat with a smile.

"So, Gabriel, I have a proposition for you. I am working on putting together a small group. It would be wonderful if you would be a part of it."

"Oh yeah, of course," Gabriel replied. He didn't even realize it, but he found himself completely trusting Pius. Then he added, "Anything you need."

"Yes, it will be sort of a club. We will be meeting in—"

But just then, Serena barged into the room. She rushed over to the desk and sat down.

"Excuse me, young lady, this is most irregular. I am in the middle of a meeting with a student."

"I know sir, but I need to speak with you immediately."

"What is this about then?" Pius asked, standing up and putting his hands down on the desk in a very put-off posture.

"I have a deadline for my article, and it's all about you," Serena said with a smile.

"Oh, really?" said Pius with a grin. "*Moi.*"

"Yes, sir," Serena said. "I need to interview you quickly and finish my article by tonight."

"Well, I supposed that would be all right."

Pius sat back down, flattening out his very expensive-looking tie. Then he pulled down at his jacket.

Serena sat down across from Pius in the chair next to Gabriel. Meanwhile, Gabriel felt like he was just waking up from a dream. The cloudiness in his mind started to clear.

"So, let's start off with a few basics. Where are you from?"

Pius answered, "Originally from Spain."

"Where in Spain?" she asked.

"A small town no one has ever heard of. Next question," he said in a buttery smooth tone.

Serena stammered for a second. "Uhhhh…" She played it off like she was just reading her notes. "How do you like working at SIA?"

Pius sat up straighter. "Oh, it is marvelous. Very accommodating staff and a dynamic facility. It is one of the best colleges in the country."

Serena's eyes shone for a second. "You mentioned the staff. Do you have any colleagues you are especially fond of or that you work with closely?"

Pius paused for a second. "Well, no one specifically."

Serena was looking at Pius, but then Gabriel noticed her hand. She was tapping her head with her hand. *Is she trying to signal me in some way*? he wondered.

"Okay then," said Serena. "What is your favorite class to teach this semester?"

Pius folded his hands together. "Well, I am particularly enjoying my Ethics class this semester." He extended a hand to Gabriel. "We have been having wonderful discussions, have we not?"

Gabriel nodded exuberantly. Just then, Gabriel heard something. His eyes bulged and he stiffened, but he tried to collect himself quickly. It was a voice, but it wasn't speaking out loud. This voice was in his head. Serena was using her telepathy. *Make an excuse and leave, okay?*

What. Why?

Just trust me, all right? she replied.

But I'm in the middle of my assignment.

This is part of the mission. Go. Wait for me downstairs.

Gabriel stood up abruptly. In a stammering voice, he said, "H—hey, Professor. I have a ton of homework. I'll see you after class."

Pius stood and extended his hand in an elaborate gesture.

Serena returned to her interview without Pius being any the wiser. "A few more questions, sir."

Gabriel exited the office and made his way down the hall. Instead of going to the bottom floor, he meandered around the offices, all the while keeping an eye on the door.

When Serena exited Pius' office, Gabriel ducked out of sight. He turned a corner and waited for her but kept an ear out for her. He could hear Pius say, "Serena, I would love to speak more. If you aren't busy tomorrow, why don't you come speak with me? I have a special group I'm starting, and I think you are just the kind of person we are looking for. Have a wonderful day."

Serena said goodbye and left. When she rounded the corner, Gabriel grabbed her arm. She almost let out a scream, but she covered her mouth. She asked Gabriel what he was doing.

Whispering, Gabriel answered, "I wanted to keep an eye on you."

"Me? You're the one almost getting mind-controlled!"

FILE #16

JOIN THE UNDERGROUND

"What do you mean?" asked Gabriel.

Serena looked at him and then back at the office. "Let's get out of here, and I'll explain."

The two of them made their way downstairs and out of the faculty tower. They walked down the walkway and into a field away from others. "Let's keep walking," she said, pulling Gabriel with her. Their hands were interlocked as she pulled him. He looked down and flushed.

He shook his head, trying to focus. Her hand was soft and warm. He found himself enjoying holding it. *No, focus*, he said to himself. "So, what did you mean up there?" he finally asked.

"Pius was…well. So, I was, uh," Serena stammered, unusually flummoxed. She turned and composed herself. "I was outside listening in on your conversation."

"When you say listening in, do you mean with your ears or your telepathy?" asked Gabriel.

Serena's eyes darted away and her face was touched with a tinge of pink. "Uh, both."

Gabriel sneered somewhat playfully. He gave her a look that said *spill it now*.

"Hey, if I wasn't using my gift, you would be a zombie-vegetable-person, okay? Pius was doing something as he was talking to you. Didn't you feel it?"

"What do you mean?" he asked, his expression morphing back into a serious one.

As they passed another crosswalk, they paused until out of earshot of the students there. "Pius was doing something. It wasn't outright telepathy or mind control, but whatever his gift is, he was doing something to you."

"What do you mean it wasn't telepathy? If it wasn't that, then what do you think it was?"

"I'm no expert, but the whole time he was talking to you, he was thinking about manipulating you. About making you another one of his disciples."

"Disciples. What? No way. He's a good guy."

Serena stopped and grabbed his shoulder. "I'm serious, Gabriel. When you were talking to him, how did you feel?"

"I don't know. He's a nice guy. I guess I felt good talking to him. That doesn't make him our enemy."

"No, you're right, it doesn't. But if he is able to manipulate people and make them do what he wants, he is infinitely more dangerous than we thought."

Gabriel looked into Serena's eyes, and he saw something there. Something like concern, but it was more than that. He couldn't put his finger on it, but it made him feel warm inside. It made his heart flutter as she stared at him. Finally, he started to nod in agreement with what Serena was saying.

***

Meanwhile, across campus, Jake was walking around kicking a stone down a side alleyway. His hands were deep in his pockets and his shoulders were sunken. He stopped around the corner of the building and leaned against it, sighing deeply. His phone buzzed in his pocket. He pulled it out, thinking it was a friend. However, it was just an email from one of his classes, notifying him that grades were being posted on their last test. He sighed and walked on.

A few minutes later, Lucien rushed down the sidewalk in Jake's direction. Lucien walked with purpose, as if he was going somewhere. Jake looked up and caught his eye. Jake put his slim device into his pocket, and he stepped in Lucien's direction.

"Well, if it isn't the flaming wonder," Lucien said with his thick accent, pronouncing the "w" like a "v" in his sentence.

Jake laughed. "How you doing?"

"What do you mean 'how you doing'? I got kicked off the team and my girlfriend broke up with me. This is the worst week of my life. I just can't wait to graduate and leave this place. I have a job lined up with one of the major energy companies. With my electricity gift, I am going to be a rich man."

"That's right," he said. "That's a shame, friend."

"Things are pretty rough right now, but I'll bounce back."

"How would you like to bounce back right now?" Jake asked.

"Right now? Sounds too good to be true," Lucien answered.

"I just joined this group. I think it might be good for you too."

Lucien and Jake started walking in the same direction. Lucien's tense expression started to fade away as Jake spoke to him.

"Maybe this group would be good for me. Help me get my priorities straight."

"Yeah, it would be perfect for you. I'm heading there if you want to come," said Jake.

Lucien's head spun for a second. "What? Right now?"

"Yeah, I think it would really help you."

"Sure, what is it called?"

"It's called the Underground."

FILE #17

THE CONCERT

The following afternoon, when Gabriel arrived at his science class, Serena already had the workstation put together for their experiment.

"Well aren't you productive?" he said jokingly.

"I couldn't help it. I have had this nervous energy all day," she said in a low voice.

Gabriel leaned in. "Because of the mission?" he asked.

"Yes," she answered. "I think Pius is our guy."

A student walked past and Gabriel pretended to be mixing some chemicals. When the student passed, Gabriel made a shushing motion to Serena as if to say *we will talk about this later*.

Meanwhile, Jake was just getting to class. "Hey," said Serena. Then she made a motion for Gabriel to look toward the door. He saw Jake walking in, looking more chipper than usual.

"Hey, folks, what are we working on today?" Jake asked.

As if in answer, Professor Shepherd started a slideshow of the process that they would be following today. It appeared from the slides that they would be making a sort of acidic compound to test the effects of corrosion on certain materials. Each student was supposed to record their results individually for the assignment.

As the group began putting their chemicals together and getting the chemical compound ready, Professor Shepherd made the rounds, watching their progress. Before making his way to Gabriel's group, he stopped to chat with another group. Within earshot, Gabriel could hear him changing the conversation to his newest book.

"You know, this reminds me of the book I am currently working on,"

Gabriel couldn't help but roll his eyes. Then something else caught his attention.

"Why don't I use my ability to just start the Bunsen burner?" Jake asked.

Meanwhile, Simon, who was the acting teacher's assistant was walking around the classroom. As Simon walked past their group, he noticed what was going on. "That's not a good idea."

"Why not?" Jake asked.

Serena chimed in. "Lots of reasons."

"There's gas emitted into the air from the device. It wouldn't be a safe choice to have an open flame near it," Simon answered.

Hearing Simon explain the situation to Jake gave Gabriel a sense of hope. With a deep sigh of relief, Gabriel walked over to the shelf nearby. Then all of a sudden, the sound of something shattering followed by a roar erupted behind him. For a brief moment, he could feel heat on the back of his neck. He dropped to the ground in response, following what his father had taught him.

He looked over his shoulder to see a fire surrounding Jake, Simon, and Serena. Gabriel immediately knew what happened. Jake hadn't listened. Meanwhile, Professor Shepherd was running from the room, calling for help and screaming about how the fire sprinklers weren't working.

Several students approached with their phones in their hands. Gabriel screamed for them to back up and vacate the room as safely as they could. He pushed through the crowd of kids, making his way toward the fire as they moved away from it.

As he reached the flames, he surrounded himself with telekinetic energy. He had a lot of experience shielding himself from Jake's fires last year, so he was quite sure he could handle this. He breathed deeply and jumped through the fire.

Simon and Serena were standing near each other with Jake trying to shield them with his flame-retardant body. Gabriel couldn't hear them, but the group was saying something. Just as he approached, Simon's eyes glowed. Then a small burst of water from the sprinklers above doused them. In just a few seconds, the flames were gone.

"Is everyone all right?" asked Gabriel.

"Yeah, we're good," answered Serena.

"That was trickier than I expected," said Simon, completely oblivious to Gabriel's question.

Looking at Jake, Gabriel asked, "What was that all about?"

"I was just…using my gift, man. We're allowed to use our gifts," Jake said.

"Not if it puts people in harm's way!"

"Hey, our gifts are meant to be used. It's how we distinguish who we are as people and as the gifted."

Serena stepped in between them. "Hey, it was an accident. It's all right."

"It isn't all right. Burn it all! Someone could have been hurt. Simon told you not to do that."

Jake stepped forward in a domineering stance. "He isn't my boss, and neither are you." Then he turned and pushed through the group, shouldering Gabriel as he passed. Gabriel looked at him, glaring intensely.

Serena put her hand on his shoulder. "That could have gone more smoothly."

He turned to look at her, still with an angry expression on his face. "So, I am the bad guy here?"

"No, but you could have handled that more tactfully."

Meanwhile, Simon was examining the workstation. The flame-retardant counter was completely fine, minus a little bit of ash. He made sure there was no potential for a second blaze. Regardless, he was completely oblivious to the tense disagreement going on beside him.

Gabriel rolled his eyes. "Seriously. How are you two so calm after that?"

Simon answered, "Jake did shield us from the fire. Once I got the sprinkler system under control, it was just a matter of getting the right ones to turn off and spray the area where we were standing. I didn't want to ruin the whole class' work."

Gabriel ran his hand down his face as if to say, *What are you talking about?* "Simon, Jake was in the wrong here," Gabriel said. "He could have hurt someone with that stupid move."

A few moments later, Shepherd returned to the room, more composed and dismissed the class for the afternoon.

As Gabriel packed his stuff together, Katrina approached him. "I saw what you did in class," she said in a timid voice.

"Huh?" Gabriel asked. At first, he hadn't noticed her. "Oh."

"I saw how you jumped in there to help your friends. That was really cool."

He blushed a smidge. "Thanks."

"Are you going to the concert?" she asked.

"Yeah," he answered. "Simon got us tickets early."

***

That evening, Gabriel met up with Serena and they walked to Simon's dorm room. As they walked down the hallway, Serna said, "I just don't see why we need to get there that early."

"He says we should get their early," Gabriel replied.

"But we have tickets already," she retorted.

"He said it is important that we get there before the line gets too long." He sighed.

"But we have reserved seats, so it is not like someone can take our spot."

As they approached the door, Gabriel said, "I didn't say it made sense. But you know how Simon gets. I think it would just ease his mind if we got there early."

Serena sighed as Gabriel knocked on the door, her ever-logical nature clearly showing. Serena didn't like things that were impractical or illogical. Simon immediately came to the door dressed for the show. "You guys are late," he said with a note of panic in his voice.

Gabriel shot a look at Serena, who fortunately bit her lip. Serena said, "Well let's hurry over there then," her voice only slightly sarcastic.

"Where's Jake?" asked Simon.

"I don't know," said Serena. "We should probably wait for him."

The group stood at the door to wait for Jake. Simon sent him several messages with his phone, not only text messages, but video and voice messages as well. As they stood at the door for a few minutes, Gabriel had a thought. "Do you think he's still mad about what happened in class?"

Serena said, "He can be a hothead, but he usually calms down after a few hours."

Finally, Simon's anxiety got the best of him. "Let's just text him that we'll be going down to the auditorium and we will wait for him there."

"Sounds like a plan," answered Gabriel. Serena rolled her eyes.

They made their way to the auditorium where the concert was being held. Serena did her best to not bring up how impossibly early they were arriving. But, whenever Simon would bring it up, she would make snarky comments. No matter how sarcastic she was, Simon was oblivious.

Once they arrived, they waited at the entrance. As they waited for the next twenty minutes, the line began to grow and grow. It eventually started to wrap around the building.

"Hey, there's Jake."

"Why is he hanging out with Lucien?" asked Serena.

Gabriel furrowed his brow. "I'm not sure. I thought they didn't get along."

"Does anyone get along with Lucien?" Simon asked. At first Gabriel thought he was making a joke, but his expression was completely serious.

"Let's ask him," Serena said. Jake was walking in their direction, but he was going toward the back of the line. "Hey, Jake. We got your ticket!" she yelled.

When he approached them, he said, "I'm going to sit with Lucien."

Gabriel said, "But we have been planning this for a while. I thought we were going to sit together."

Jake shrugged, like he didn't want to talk about it, and walked off with Lucien. Gabriel stood with hands out in a posture of uncertainty. *What's going on with Jake?* he wondered.

After a long wait, the three friends were allowed to enter. Because they were so close to the front of the line, they were able to make it inside before the pushing and shoving got too bad. Simon kept remarking that this was why he wanted to get their early. Each time he did so, Serena rolled her eyes harder and harder. Gabriel was pretty sure they would roll right out of her head pretty soon.

Simon pulled out his device and found the digital tickets. They were scanned and then the group was allowed inside the arena. The main concourse was a swarm of people, and they almost lost Simon because he was moving so quickly. Fortunately, they were able to keep enough of an eye on him so that they didn't get separated. They made their way to their seats, and they were actually very good seats, three rows back and close to the center. As they sat, Simon remarked that these were better than the front row because they had a better view of the show. Serena feigned a nod of agreement.

"You may need some eye drops with all the eye rolling you're doing tonight," Gabriel whispered.

"Yeah, and the hanger in my mouth from this fake smile is not comfortable either," she replied.

The seats around them began to fill up. The show was really going to be a packed event. In what felt like no time, the show was starting. The crowds started to cheer as the lights dimmed. Colored stage lights flared to life in a rainbow of colors. But then Gabriel realized they weren't stage lights. A woman walked out of the shadows and was creating captivating light shows from her hands. She made the colors dance in the air and lights dazzled the eyes.

The rest of the band made their way out onto the stage. As they grabbed their instruments, fog covered the stage. Gabriel noticed a gifted manipulating the fog as it danced and swirled around the band members. The guitarist started strumming on his guitar and then started an impossible progression of notes. He held his hand out over the guitar, making it literally sing. The big screen to the side showed the audience that he wasn't playing it with his fingers. He was playing it with his mind. The sounds were mesmerizing.

Then the drummer kicked on his bass drum, and the rest of the band fell into a sweet rhythm. There were no amplifiers or any kind of sound devices on the stage. Over to the left, he saw a girl holding out her hands. The sounds were being projected from her. Somehow, she was manipulating and even amplifying the sounds of each instrument. Then she started singing, and Gabriel realized she was the lead singer. Not only that, but she was able to manipulate sound itself.

The band was putting on a fantastic performance. After the eighth or ninth song, Gabriel went to grab some water from the concession stand. He went up the stairs to the main level and turned a corner. The first two he passed had lines that were impossibly long, so he passed them and looked for another. He came to a shorter one when he bumped into Jake. Jake was standing in line. Gabriel approached him, hoping to talk.

"Uh, hey, dude," Gabriel started with a tinge of anxiety.

Jake turned around and rolled his eyes. "What's going on?"

"Hey, can we talk about what happened in the science lab?" Gabriel asked.

"Listen dude. It's fine. I gotta get back to the show."

"Wait, I just wanted to say—"

Jake interrupted him. "No, just let it go." Jake left the line and walked in the opposite direction. Gabriel started to follow him, feeling uncertain.

"Dude, wait. What's wrong?" Gabriel asked, trying to catch up to him.

With a sigh, Jake answered, "Nothing is wrong." He kept walking without turning toward Gabriel. "Just leave me alone, all right?"

Gabriel moved forward to catch up with Jake, which was harder than expected with the sprawling crowd of people moving in every direction. Finally, he caught up to Jake and put his hand on his shoulder, stopping him. Jake turned around with bulging eyes and gritted teeth. Gabriel's eyes widened at his dark expression. It shocked Gabriel to see his friend respond in such an aggressive manner.

"I just wanted to..." Gabriel started but trailed off when he saw Jake's hand. Small embers licked at his fingers and his hand was clenched in a fist. That was when a thought hit Gabriel. Gabriel hadn't heard him snap. Maybe it was because the loud music in the distance, but he was unsure. *Was Jake going to attack him?*

Jake pulled his shoulder away from Gabriel. He turned and walked away as Gabriel just stood there. People pushed past him. A group crowded him and he was jostled left and right. But he didn't leave that spot. He stood there, gazing in Jake's direction, watching him become swallowed by the crowd and then disappear.

What just happened? he thought.

FILE # 18

A QUESTION OF GREATNESS

The following morning, Gabriel went to practice. He usually opted for the morning practice because it was less crowded. Most of the team chose to sleep in. Gabriel was using his telekinesis to lift different weights in succession.

While in the weight room with Claudio, Derek barged into the room in something of a huff. Claudio, who was doing deadlifts, dropped his weights. The impact shook the floor. Meanwhile, Derek slammed the locker room door, causing the hinges to loosen and it fell off the wall.

Gabriel and Claudio made eye contact. Claudio nodded his head toward the locker room. Gabriel put his weights down using his mind as he walked away. Each one fit into its specific slot and rested nicely.

Claudio went first, with Gabriel right on his heels. They peeked their head around the corner and saw Derek putting on his weight-lifting gloves as he mumbled to himself.

"W-what's a matter there, big fella?" he asked. "You don't seem to be your normal, radiant self."

Derek thumped his hands onto the counter, his massive arms like pillars holding his weight. Gabriel rounded the corner and leaned against the counter. "You all right?" he asked.

"What's wrong with your friend?" Derek asked, still looking down at the sink.

Claudio and Gabriel looked at each other once again, unsure of whom he was speaking to. Claudio pointed at Gabriel and then back at himself a few times.

"He must mean you," Claudio whispered. "Because all of my friends are awesome."

"I don't know," Gabriel murmured back. "Could be either of us."

Then Derek started talking again. "I went to the Colombiana this morning to get my regular on my cheat day."

Both of the boys nodded.

"And guess who was there making a scene?"

Neither Claudio or Gabriel answered. Although Gabriel was starting to suspect he knew who Derek was referring to.

"Jake Burns. That surfer-looking wannabe was mad about the coffee he ordered. He was screaming and hollering like a burning fool."

He paused.

"So, I go over to him and ask him what is going on, and he gives me this," Derek said as he turned to face Claudio and Gabriel. He pointed to his face. He left eye was swollen and marred by a bruise.

"He punched you?" asked Claudio.

"Yeah, that little…" Derek bit his tongue. He looked at Gabriel. "Listen, I know that he's your friend. But something is definitely wrong with that guy." Then Derek pushed forward and walked past them out of the locker room. From a distance they heard him say, "Tell Coach I'll fix that door after I work out this frustration."

Claudio turned to Gabriel, his finger on his nose. "Not it."

Gabriel rolled his eyes and walked out of the locker room.

***

Pius had let the kids skip class the day after the concert. It was just another reason so many of the kids fawned over him. But it also meant one more day that Gabriel couldn't gain any intelligence on him.

In the next class, Gabriel was sitting next to Zoey and telling her about practice. She asked him about what happened to Derek, so he told her.

"He could get himself kicked off the team for that. Is Derek going to report him?" she asked.

"I don't know," he answered.

Just then, Pius came down the stairs to his desk with Jake at his side. "Speak of the devil," said Zoey.

Gabriel watched as they walked down the stairs toward the professor's desk. When they got to the bottom, Pius spoke with Jake some more. Finally, he checked his watch. He must have told Jake that class was about to begin because Jake took a seat in the front row.

Zoey nudged Gabriel. "Since when does Jake sit in the front row?"

"Since he started taking this class, apparently."

Pius began class by telling them about how he enjoyed the recent concert. He often began class in these ways. It made him more personal than most of his professors. Then he began to say, "Well I supposed we need to begin class today, don't we?"

The class collectively laughed. He walked around his desk, sat on the corner, and looked at the class. He didn't speak, not right away. He built up the tension as he looked around the room. Then, finally, he spoke. "They say that mankind is the ruler of the world, correct?" he started. No one responded, of course. No one ever spoke out of turn at his lectures. "If mankind is the apex creature in the world, this begs a question," he said and then paused. "Are the gifted not better than regular humans?"

The room sat in stunned silence for a second.

"What do you think, are gifted better than humans?"

A short girl in the front of the room raised her hand. "I think all humans are the same, whether they are gifted or not."

Several heads nodded in agreement, and a few murmurs spread in hushed tones.

A few more hands rose.

"I don't see how gifted and non-gifted are any different," one student said.

"Didn't our founding fathers say we were all created as equals?" asked a tall kid at the back of the room.

Then Professor Pius spoke up, "Indeed, I too think that we are all created as equals, no man better than another," he said and then paused for dramatic effect. "However, as many of you know, in the years after the Transit of Venus, many groups sprang up that pushed the idea that the gifted were different and, in many respects, better than their human brothers."

The class sat in silence for a moment. Professor Pius began walking up the stairs in the center of the classroom, looking at each of the students.

"Each human being, the gifted and none, have the power to do great things, do they not?" he asked. The class all nodded in agreement. "What is it that causes greatness?" he asked next, pausing to turn around and look around the room. "Is it wealth, social standing, influence?"

One student raised their hand. "I think greatness is what we do with the opportunities we have."

"It's the ability to cause real change," said another student.

Next, Jake raised his hand and said, "I think greatness is our power. People like Alexander the Great or the Emperor of Germania."

"I think greatness is when you have the ability to do something good, and you do it."

The discussion continued for the rest of class with Pius presenting different scenarios for them. They debated all manner of greatness. Some were examples of power, others of economic success.

At the end of class, Pius turned around and faced the board. He looked at a map of the world. "This was a wonderful discussion, class. Ethics and philosophy are all about asking the hard questions. Today, we have done just that." Then he dismissed them all.

Gabriel grabbed his things and made his way down the stairs to the front row. However, Jake was already on his way up the stairs. Just as Gabriel went to open his mouth, Jake pushed past him, throwing his shoulder into Gabriel.

As Gabriel stood there, he clenched his fist, his knuckles turning white. He wanted to react; he wanted to respond. But he knew that thrashing out in anger wouldn't turn this situation around.

Professor Pius walked past Gabriel with an overcoat over one arm and a briefcase in the other. Pushing up his small glasses, Pius paused when he approached Gabriel. "Good day, Mr. Green." Then he walked away with a knowing smile. "Mr. Burns, shall I see you tonight?" he asked.

Gabriel's eyes widened. He looked at the ground while he grabbed his phone from his pocket. It was ringing. A familiar name flashed on the screen. He picked it up, and Serena's voice was on the other end of the line.

"We need to see your advisor."

FILE #19

FALLEN FIGURES

Gabriel came around the corner as he exited the building. Immediately, Serena was there, pulling him by the arm. Gabriel wasn't sure what was going on. Serena pulled him into the courtyard. Once they were away from the crowds of students, Serena turned toward Gabriel as they walked.

"All right, let's go talk to your advisor," she said looking around her to see if anyone is listening.

"Yeah, you said that," replied Gabriel.

"I know. But I just met with my 'advisor,'" she said making air quotes with her fingers. "She's leaving, but she said that she wants us to see Coach. And he'll run point of this next phase."

"Next phase?" Gabriel asked. "What do you mean, 'next phase'?"

"I told her that we have evidence that Pius is our guy, and she wants us to look into it."

While they walked toward the gymnasium, Gabriel sighed and shook his head. His first mission was not going how he imagined. He kept thinking things would go so much more smoothly than this. He thought of the old spy movies, and how the hero always knew exactly what to do. Gabriel had no idea what to do. He didn't even know if their suspect was the right guy.

When they arrived at the gymnasium, the doors were locked. They looked inside, and all of the lights were off, which was odd because the gymnasium had something of a twenty-four-hour policy.

Gabriel looked at his phone. "There should be an afternoon practice going on soon. The building shouldn't be locked."

"Something isn't right," said Serena.

"Yeah, that's odd. Does Coach know we are coming?" Gabriel asked.

"Yes. My mentor told me that Coach would be expecting us."

"Very odd."

"Can you get us inside?" Serena asked.

Gabriel looked at her with a questioning expression.

"Let's go around to the side."

The two went to a side entrance. There were bushes surrounding the door so they were mostly obscured. Gabriel used his telekinetic gifts to open the door without tripping an alarm. Serena went in first. She moved with a catlike grace that Gabriel had never seen before. It was as if she had trained for this. Now that he thought of it, Gabriel didn't know too much about Serena's upbringing.

Inside, the lights were all off, just like at the front. Small emergency lights gave off the faintest of glows. It made the hallways just visible enough to not run into anything, but outside of that, it was very dark.

Serena moved down the hallway, hugging the wall. She slid down the hall and looked around the corner. She didn't look at him, but her hand wave motioned for him to come down. Gabriel tried to copy her movement. However, she moved with much more fluid intentionality and grace. He stopped just beside her and went to whisper, but she threw her hand up to stop him.

Then Gabriel realized why she silenced him. Right as she did so, a voice entered his head. It was Serena's.

We can move onward, but don't talk.

He answered back, *Sorry about that.*

Don't worry about it. I wouldn't expect you to think like that.

He made an expression like he was hurt, but he tried to push the thought away.

They continued to move down the dark hallway. All of the rooms were empty. The weight rooms, the locker rooms, and the main arena. Everything. Finally, they made their way to the offices.

Serena opened the door, and just as she did, something smashed through the doors and sent her to the ground. Gabriel's eyes widened as two shadowy figures barged through the door. With acrobatic agility, Serena somersaulted backwards into a crouching position. Gabriel threw the first attacker back into the hallway wall with a telekinetic push.

However, the second assailant jumped for Serena before Gabriel could get to them. Instinctively, Serena rolled on the ground and the figure ran into the wall. She came around behind the figure and delivered a kick to their back, sending them into the wall and cracking the drywall. Gabriel rushed the first figure and pushed them back into the wall before they could continue their attack.

The figure, he realized, was Avery. Gabriel's eyes widened, but he couldn't let up. What Avery lacked in control, he made up for in overall energy. The air began to crackle with energy. Crimson energy surrounded Avery, and he sent out a blast at Gabriel. He deflected the shot at the ground, burning a hole in the ground. Before he could ready a second shot, Gabriel rushed him. He threw two punches that were met by a wall of plasma energy.

He made eye contact with Avery. *That's new*, he thought.

Avery surrounded himself in crimson energy and threw his own punch. Gabriel tried to block himself with his own energy.

The blow sent Gabriel back several feet but made no direct damage.

Meanwhile, Serena noticed that her combatant was a stocky youth with bushy, dark hair. He charged forward again, but Serena was able to dodge once again. However, this time when she turned around from her cartwheel, the figure disappeared. She remembered that one of the fighters on the sparring team had an invisibility gift.

"Burn it all," she said under her breath. "I should not have wasted time."

Just then, she felt a blow to her back and it pushed her down to the ground. She caught herself quickly and jumped back up in the air before another blow smashed the ground where she was moments ago. When she landed, she quickly tried to sense where he was using her telepathy.

Just as an invisible fist was coming for her face, she dodged to the left, caught the arm, wrapped her own arms around it, and used all of her body weight to drop him to the ground. Although she couldn't see his face, she could hear his thoughts. And boy, was he surprised.

The massive thud she heard was satisfying. She jumped back up to her feet. He stood up and she could hear him breathing raggedly and coughing. Before he could ready himself, she jumped and delivered a roundhouse kick to his shoulder. He had a thick frame, but he was off balance. She saw a crack appear in the drywall, and then his body appeared, half-leaning against the wall.

Down the hall, Gabriel was deflecting another burst of plasma energy. This one ricocheted into the door and blasted it off its hinges.

"That one's on you Avery," he said.

Then he had a thought. When the next blast of energy came at him, he threw all of his own energy into it and discharged it back at Avery. The blast connected with his own energy, and canceled it out for a moment. Not wasting a moment, Gabriel followed the blast and was on Avery in a second. He delivered two punches to his chest and then a telekinetic push that threw him back into the wall. This time, the drywall gave way completely and Avery dropped to the ground, covered in broken pieces and dust.

Gabriel was heaving when Serena came over to him. "Took you long enough," she whispered.

He dropped his arms to his side and then made a gesture, as if to say *well, sorry*. She looked through the doorway.

"Well, no sneaking in now, I guess."

"No kidding," Gabriel replied.

"Which way is his office?" she asked.

"It's right down this hallway," Gabriel said, indicating the direction with this hand.

They approached Coach's office. Serena moved first, with Gabriel trailing her. She peered in the window, but the blinds were down. Gabriel could see that the lights were off, but something inside was giving off a glow.

Telepathically, Serena told Gabriel, *I'm going to go in first, and you follow close behind me, all right?*

He nodded in understanding. But he realized that she wasn't looking at him. So, he replied, *Yes.*

Being impossibly quiet, Serena opened the door and slipped into the room. Gabriel followed her, attempting to mirror her quietness. However, just as he stepped down, the floorboard squealed. He rolled his eyes as they entered the office.

Inside, Gabriel could see Coach V sitting at his desk. His monitor was glowing, but Coach wasn't actually looking at the screen. He was staring off into the distance.

"Coach V, we wanted to talk to you about the *semester*," Serena said, putting extra emphasis on the word semester. "We think something is going on."

However, Coach V never looked up.

"Coach?" Gabriel asked.

"Oh, he isn't able to communicate at the moment," said a voice from behind them that caused them both to jump up with fear.

Serena and Gabriel turned to see a figure in the darkness, sitting on a chair against the far wall. He was cloaked in shadows so they hadn't seen him when they walked into the room. He walked toward them. "Funny running into you two here," said Professor Pius.

Serena eyes widened. Gabriel looked confused. Then Serena looked at Gabriel with a *told you so* look.

"I never would have expected Coach V would be an agent with the Guild," Pius said, walking around them to the desk. Then as he sat at the corner, he added, "He's so unassuming."

"What did you do to him?" asked Serena.

"Oh, him. All you need to know is that he is under my sway."

"So, you do have mind control powers!" said Gabriel with an accusatory tone.

"Well, no, not exactly Mr. Green," Pius answered in that silky-smooth voice of his. "My ability is not just mind control. It goes deeper than that. And your leader over here, he is under my control."

Gabriel, take him down!

Gabriel raised his hand, readying a telekinetic attack. But just as he did so, Pius held out a hand toward Coach V. "Make a move to harm me, and it won't end well for Coach V."

"What?" he asked.

"If I am harmed, Coach V stays in this vegetative state for the rest of his life. No more coaching; no more agent business."

Gabriel's eyes narrowed. Pius stood up, ran a hand over his hair to make sure none of it was out of place, and straightened his collar.

"Why don't the two of you join us at the Underground tonight? We're having a meeting, and it would be good to add some more young blood to our numbers."

Serena sneered at him. "You can't get away with this, Pius. You know that, right? There are plenty of agents we can ca—"

But just then, Serena was cut off when Pius held up his hand. "That's where you are wrong. I have made sure my associate here has blocked all communications with your teams." As he was speaking, another figure walked out of the shadows. Pius put his hand on the man's shoulder.

"I believe you know this young man, correct?" As he said that, the silhouette stepped forward and the computer screen's glow shone on his face. It was Simon. "Simon has made sure that no back-up will be coming to help you two."

Serena and Gabriel's eyes widened.

"My offer still stands, you know? You honestly have no other choice. You can come with me and be on the winning side. Or you could turn around and walk away. I hope you will make the right choice and join us. Don't you want to be on the winning side?"

The two looked at each other. Serena's face fell. Millions of ideas raced through her mind. Meanwhile, Gabriel looked contemplative. He was thinking what they should do.

Pius grabbed a fine rain coat from the chair, and he draped it over his arm. "Well, gentlemen, shall we be off then? Come along."

As he said this, both Coach V and Simon stood up and followed Pius out of the door. As he left, Pius waved and closed the door behind them, keeping an arrogantly calm demeanor. Gabriel could hear their footsteps as they walked down the hallway.

Serena looked at Gabriel. "What do we do?" she asked.

"I have no idea. Do you think he is right?"

She looked shocked. "What do you mean? Of course, he isn't right. We can't just let him get away with our friends. With my...fost—I mean, Coach."

Gabriel looked at her, confused. She saw his expression and realized he caught what she said. She ran her hand through her long red hair in exasperation. "Look, Coach V and I have a pretty unique relationship."

"How so?" asked Gabriel.

"Well, he essentially raised me."

FILE #20

INTO THE UNDERGROUND

Gabriel sat there in shock for a moment. Finally, he stuttered, "W-what do you mean he raised you?"

"I haven't told anyone this, but my parents were agents. My father died when I was pretty young, but my mom…" She paused for a moment. "She was on a mission with Coach V. I guess things went bad, and she isn't coming back. He felt responsible for what happened to my parents, and he became my foster dad. He's raised me since then."

"Wow, I mean, I just…wow…well…I never knew."

"Of course, you didn't. Like I said, I haven't told anyone that before," she said and paused again. "It's…well…It's kind of a sore subject for me."

"Yeah, right. Of course, it is. I am sorry."

Gabriel didn't know what to say. He wasn't very good in these emotional situations. It was like his mind went completely blank.

"So…uh, I guess that we need to figure out how to get into the Underground," he finally said after a long, awkward pause.

"I mean, he invited us in, didn't he?" Serena replied.

Gabriel nodded, catching onto what she said. "Hmm, you're right. So, what, we act like we are interested?"

"Exactly."

"Then what?" he asked.

"We get to Pius, and we find a way to break his hold on our friends. But first, I need to call us some backup."

Gabriel looked confused. "What do you mean? Pius said he made sure no backup would come."

"True. But he is banking on us trying to use technology, and I'm not using technology."

"So, you are going to contact your advisor?" he asked.

"No, she's out of range for my current ability. So, we will have to contact someone on campus."

"Who?" Gabriel asked.

"Don't you worry, I know a guy," she answered.

***

Serena and Gabriel approached the building. Gabriel had this feeling of déjà vu. He couldn't quite put his finger on it. Was it because he'd been here before, or was it the similarity of the situation? For the second time, he was being led by someone who was actually much more involved than he ever realized. *Were all of his friends secretly agents?*

At the entrance, Serena took the lead. Two students stood at the entrance. A tall, muscular young man with a shaved head and a girl with a scowl on her face. She had a tablet in her hand. Serena walked straight up to them and told the girl that Pius had sent for them.

The girl made an unimpressed look and looked at her tablet. Then she looked at the other gatekeeper and nodded. He unlocked the door and let them into the compound. Inside, it was just like before, although it did look as if more work had been done. The air was thick with sawdust and heavy paint fumes. Many of the walls were refinished and some of the floors were partially swept.

Just then, Lucien stopped them. "What are you two doing here?" he asked in his thick European accent.

"Pius invited us. We are here to see him."

As if he didn't hear her statement, Lucien looked at the two guards at the door. "You two head to your rooms and pack up," he told them. Then looking back at Serena, he said, "I'll lead you down to his chambers. Please, follow me."

"Could I use the restroom, first?" she asked.

Lucien looked unusually annoyed by this, but he showed her to a restroom. Meanwhile, Gabriel and Lucien stood outside, looking awkwardly at each other.

"So, you, uh…you come here often?" asked Gabriel.

Lucien didn't reply. Instead, he rolled his eyes. Seconds later, Serena exited the restroom.

"Did you boys get along while I was out?" she asked.

Not wanting to reply, Lucien just said, "Let us go."

Lucien took them down the stairs to a dark cellar. In the dimly lit hallway, they turned the opposite way they came before and went down to a large door. The large door had a massive lock over it. From the looks of it, this was probably a storage room for frozen foods back when the building was originally built.

Lucien approached the door and typed a quick succession of numbers on the digital keypad. The keypad contrasted the old door and looked like it was just installed, whereas the door looked to be quite old. Once he finished the code, the door opened. Lucien grabbed the large chrome handle and pulled the door open. With the door ajar, Lucien motioned for them to enter. Serena walked forward first with confidence, and Gabriel followed, looking at Serena. He found her air of confidence attractive.

The room was like a stone block. The walls were void of any decor or ornamentation. The room was lit by a few scattered, dim lights. The far wall had two windows that were covered in black paint. Inside, a man with dark hair sat on a large chair, his salt and peppered locks giving him away.

Beside him was Jake. But it wasn't Jake. It wasn't the Jake that Gabriel knew. His eyes were not the same as before. His expression was angrier than normal.

Pius stood up and held out his hands. He clapped and looked at Gabriel sardonically. "Well, well, well. Look who it is."

Serena walked toward Pius's direction across the room. Two students flanked him on the right and left, and as Serena approached, they jumped in front of him as if they were bodyguards. She stopped as the two students blocked her progress.

"It's fine my children," he said with that usual arrogance. "These two are here for a reason."

He approached her as she stood at the center of the room, not completely closing the distance that separated them. He looked at her with a strange intensity. It was as if he was gauging her. Sizing her up, maybe. From Gabriel's perspective, it was like two powerful creatures fighting for dominance, fighting for who was actually in charge of this situation. On one hand, Pius had the obvious upper hand in the situation. He had Lucien, Simon, Jake, Coach V, and two unknown students under his control. But on the other hand, Gabriel was certain that Serena had a plan. She also had the one gift that could undermine Pius's whole operation.

Gabriel stood a few feet behind Serena and surveyed the room. Serena and Pius stood about ten feet apart, glaring at each other. In the far corner, Simon and Coach V stood in a dazed stupor. Jake looked from the throne with a murderous grin. *How was this all going to go down?*

As if in answer to Gabriel's question, Pius spoke first, his power play to make sure he was in control of the situation. "Well, Serena. Gabriel. You two are here because you've made a decision, I presume. I trust it is the right one."

"Of course. We know we are in no position to bargain with you. We decided that the best option was to partner up with you."

Pius's tense shoulders slackened. He straightened his collar and drew up his tie. "Indeed. If you had not come willingly, you would have been dragged here by force. This way is so much easier on everyone," he said with an air of tenderness. As always, Pius spoke as if he was doing them a favor.

"Yes, sir," she said.

Pius looked back at Lucien, still standing at the door. "Have the rest of the grunts gone back to their dorms to prepare for our departure?"

"Yes, I sent the last two when they arrived," he answered motioning to Gabriel and Serena.

"Very well. We are all set for our migration then. I supposed all that is left to do is initiate these two."

Serena spoke up. "What migration, sir?"

"Well, I don't need this job or this school anymore. I have chosen the ten strongest members of my Underground, and I will take control of what should be mine."

Gabriel could see Serena's expression. Her eyes widened, a look of pain in them and tears welled up in them. She batted her eyes to keep them from getting any wetter, and she composed herself so as not to give away their plan.

"Who wants to go first?" Pius asked.

"I will, sir," she answered before Gabriel could even think about answering. "But can I ask how it all works? Having an ability like I do, I've always wondered how it's done."

"Hmm, always the intellectual, Miss Harmon," he said, going into his usual elaborate speech, just like he did in the classroom. "My ability is empathic manipulation. If I can gauge a person's emotions, then I can manipulate them with a high level of precision."

"So, you pretty much mind-control the students?"

"In a way, but it is almost better than mind control. Because it is not mental, the emotional the effects are almost stronger. You see, human beings are intelligent creatures, yes. But they are much more driven by emotion than by logical thought." As Pius spoke, he walked closer to Serena.

"So, whereas my ability allows me to understand the mind, your ability lets you read emotions?" she asked.

Now, Pius was beside her. He put his arm on her shoulder. "Yes, our abilities are like two sides of the same coin. Very similar, but affecting different parts of the body. You can control the mind, where I can control the emotions."

"Interesting," she replied. "Well, I guess I'm ready, sir."

"Very well," he answered, and he began to focus on her emotions, shaping them to his will. "Serena, tell me, why are you so angry?"

With tears in her eyes, she looked up at him. "Because you took the man who helped raise me."

The sound of glass shattering filled the air.

FILE #21

BROTHERS IN ARMS

As Serena was staring down Pius, Gabriel realized the small window actually was shattered. Although he hadn't even realized it, but he had instinctively moved to cover his face. But as he looked over, he saw a dark shadow, kneeling there in all black. It had dark black hair pulled back into a pony tail. Blinking, Gabriel looked and started to recognize this figure.

She started to rise, and Gabriel realized it was Jin. Jin made it to her feet and looked over at Lucien, who wasn't that far from her. Pius immediately looked over at Jin. "What is going on here?" Pius looked back at Serena, who was smirking. He stood up straight, once again regaining his composure. He smoothed back his hair and straightened his suit jacket. "Ah, I understand. You never intended to join us, did you?"

"Nope," Serena answered with a devilish grin.

"Well, I supposed we will need to move to Plan B," he said in a calm tone. He noticed her smile, and replied with his own.

"Why in the world are you smiling? We have the clear advantage. You're outmatched and outmanned."

"Well, you will forgive me if we try anyway," she answered.

"If that is how you want it. Lucien, would you take care of our uninvited guest?" he said, more of a command than a question. Lucien immediately took to attacking Jin.

Then Pius looked back at Jake. However, he held a hand out toward Gabriel. "Jake, here he is. The man who keeps you down. The one who purposefully overshadows you."

"No, Jake, don't listen to him!"

"Why not, Gabriel?" Pius asked. "Because you know I'm telling him the truth?"

"No, you are filling his head with lies! You're twisting things!"

Pius walked behind Jake with a hand on his shoulder. He pointed at Gabriel with his other hand. "I haven't twisted anything. I have been a friend when you were too busy being the hero to be there for your friend."

"Jake..." Gabriel said in a voice just above a whisper. "No..."

Jake's chest began to heave. His breath was speeding up. Then the corner of his lip began to tremble. Gabriel noticed his hand begin to twitch. Then his fingers balled into fists. Pius patted him on the back and turned his back to him.

"Finish him, Jake."

Jake rushed at Gabriel with a ferocious speed and threw the first punch. As he did so, Gabriel heard a snap. He threw up a shield, and a flame-engulfed hand crashed into it. With wide eyes, Gabriel looked at Jake.

"You've been getting stronger, haven't you, Jake?" Gabriel asked.

"Of course. Because you stole my spot on the team, I had to find a new place to train. Lucky for me, Professor Pius took me in. Now, I am stronger than ever." Jake snapped again with his opposite hand, and a torrent of fire erupted from his fingers. The flames bloomed around him like a flower. Each flame was a deadly petal. Jake was at the center. Gabriel stood back with his feet apart. He centered himself ready for Jake's next attack. Taking a cue from Jake, Gabriel began to surround himself in telekinetic energy. The energy surrounded his arms and hands, just like Jake with his fire.

As expected, Jake rushed at Gabriel. His arms were still roaring with fire. Jake's left fist thrashed at Gabriel. Moving into a defensive posture, Gabriel's arm parried the attack and deflected it back. However, a second punch was already on its way. This one struck home and hit Gabriel's shoulder.

The white-hot blaze was enough to make him want to pass out. Gabriel pulled back, and a hole in his shirt revealed a searing wound. His right shoulder throbbed. The pain wracked his body and he dropped to a knee.

Jake stood over him. He looked down at Gabriel. There was something different about him. It was his eyes. Gabriel noticed his eyes were different. Normally his eyes were a shining gold, but they looked different now.

Jake put his foot to Gabriel's chest. He kicked him down to the ground. As he hit the ground, dust shot up into the air. A thick, black powder filled his nostrils. His wound stung from the ash-like dust. Gabriel started coughing.

Gabriel rolled backward and onto his feet, several feet away from Jake. "It doesn't have to be like this, Jake!"

"I think it does," Jake answered.

"You were like a brother to me, Jake."

Jake rushed at Gabriel. His technique didn't change. Even though he was stronger, Jake favored a fast and aggressive style of combat. His style was in direct opposition to Gabriel's, who took a defensive technique.

This time, when Jake threw his one-two punch, Gabriel used a maneuver he learned from Jin. When Jake punched, Gabriel stepped into the attack and caught Jake with an elbow to the chest. Then, in one quick motion, he threw Jake over his shoulder. Because of his momentum, Jake soared through the air. He careened to the ground with a massive thud. His body slid several inches, leaving a human-shaped impression in the dust.

"Jake, I don't want to fight my brother." Tears began welling up in Gabriel's eyes. "Stop this. You're my brother."

Jake stood up. His face was twisted in a mask of pain. Confusion started to etch his face. He shook his head and pushed long, blond hair out of his face.

"Please, Jake. I don't want to fight you."

For a moment, Gabriel thought that Jake would stop. In that moment, he looked at Gabriel with something like compassion. Then he stepped forward. A shadow covered his face. But even in the shadow, Gabriel could see those golden eyes. But that was when Gabriel noticed what was different about his eyes. They didn't look gold anymore. They looked old and faded, more like tarnished brass than gold.

With his next step, Jake was out of the shadows, and he stood in front of Gabriel. His body tense and rigid. Gabriel had hoped he had gotten to him, but his body language didn't look like someone who was willing to bury the hatchet.

Jake threw up a hand with lightning quick reflexes and shot a bolt of fire at Gabriel. Gabriel shielded himself like before. But unlike the normal attack, this one exploded. Gabriel was sent flying back. He sailed through the air for what felt like hours. Then he crashed into the ground, sliding back several more feet.

He sat up against the far wall. His eyes were fuzzy and his mind was dazed. He noticed Jake in front of him. He was saying something, but Gabriel couldn't hear him. Jake grabbed him by his shirt and lifted him up. He was yelling in Gabriel's face. Still fazed by the blast, Gabriel couldn't understand what Jake was saying. Then he noticed an intense and intolerable ringing in his ears. Finally, Gabriel realized he was deafened by the explosion.

Jake was still yelling. Spittle sprayed Gabriel's face. His left eye didn't want to open all the way. Things were not looking good for Gabriel in that moment. He knew he needed to do something, but what could he do?

A powerful punch knocked the air out of Gabriel. Like a deflated balloon, Gabriel fell to the ground. Jake stood over him. He turned around and walked away. Meanwhile, Gabriel sat on the ground coughing up red spittle into his hand.

He looked at Jake, who was now in the center of the room. Inside, Gabriel was wrecked by a fear that this was going to be his end. He was not as strong as Jake, and the fact that Jake had this reckless rage about him made this fight a one-sided affair. Fear filled him so much he felt like he would drown in all of that terror.

When he caught his breath, Gabriel stood up. His hands were shaking and his eyes seemed glassy. His heart was racing a million miles a second. He tried to hide how he felt on the inside. Jake looked at him with those eyes filled with rage. He was like a barbarian rampaging with no regard for anyone or anything.

"That's it, Jake!" called Pius. "Use that rage. Use that hatred."

Jake sneered at Gabriel.

"Finish him!" Pius yelled.

Serena stepped in between Pius and Jake. She stared at him with cold eyes. "You need to end this, professor."

"Professor," he responded with a scoffing laugh. "As far as the title of professor, you can drop the pretense. To original point, I cannot surrender now. Not when things are going so well for me." Then Pius turned to where Coach V was standing looking like a zombie next to Simon. "Why don't I have these two fight each other to the death?" he asked her in a sadistic tone.

Serena looked at him with disgust and terror. "I won't let you."

"How can you stop me?" he asked. "You aren't as good with your ability as I am with mine. I came from nothing, and it was my gift that got me to where I am now."

Serena held out her hand and focused her mind on Pius. She focused on trying to break the connection he had on Coach V and Simon.

Pius sensed what she was doing. "What do you think you are doing?" he asked with a smile.

"I'm going to break the link you have with them. I'll sever it and free them."

Pius laughed out loud. "That's not how it works, young one. I don't have a connection with them. I have gained control of them by learning their emotions and gaining control of their emotions. Once I have control of their emotions, I essentially control them."

Just as he said that, the fight between Gabriel and Jake was shifting. This drew Pius's attention toward them.

Serena understood that. She knew that people, being emotional creatures, used their hearts much more than their heads to act. But she could still communicate with them, and maybe she could get them to fight to break his control.

Without looking at them, she focused her mind on communicating with Coach V. *Coach, it's me, Serena. I need you to fight this control. You are strong enough to fight this.*

Coach's voice railed back at her. *No, I am not. It is my fault that your parents are gone. Pius showed me that. He helped me understand that I am not a leader.*

Coach, that's not true. That mission wasn't your fault.

It was, though. I am the reason they were put in that position. I should have seen what was happening.

Serena tried to refrain from showing emotion. She didn't want to tip Pius off to what she was doing. But still, she spoke with Coach in her mind. *Coach V, you know that you aren't to blame. That mission went bad because of Agent Gamut, not you.*

Maybe if I had been better, I would have seen it coming. I would have known the risk of using Agent Gamut. But I didn't. My gift failed me.

Coach V, I don't blame you. You were like a father to me. You need to let go of that guilt. I forgive you.

With that, Coach V felt a shift in his mind. It was as if the emotions that were causing him to lock up and not move were gone. He shook his head. Then he looked at Serena. He mouthed the words, *Do you really?*

Without speaking, she said, *I do.*

FILE #22

BROTHERS IN SCARS

Obeying Pius's order, Jake rushed Gabriel, closing the distance with amazing speed. Gabriel knew that he had to do something quick. Without thought, he just reacted. As Jake moved in recklessly, Gabriel made his right hand in a white-knuckled fist. Just as he did, Jake also threw a punch.

Both fists connected at the same moment. Jake and Gabriel's fists each slammed the other boys face, just under the right eye. They each stumbled and fell back. Gabriel fell back into the wall while Jake fell back onto the ground and collided into a pillar. For several seconds, they both sat there, panting and heaving.

Get up, Jake! came a voice inside his head. But it was not his own voice. It was Pius'. *This is the boy who scorned you. He belittled you, and he betrayed you.*

Jake wasn't moving much, and Gabriel was trying to think of some way to win this fight. Jake was not going to stay down for long. He didn't want to hurt Jake, but Jake seemed to not share that ideal. So, he would have to find some way to stop Jake without hurting him, some way to overcome his mind control.

Just then an idea came to him. Gabriel remembered what Coach V talked to him about in his office. He remembered the story about the agents. About that mission. But more importantly, about the tele-stasis field.

***

Meanwhile, Jin was dodging another arc of lightning from Lucien. The smell of ozone filled the air. Lucien held his hands out, once again wearing his magnetic bracelets. The same ones that he was kicked off of the team for wearing. They helped him augment his ability.

Lucien held his arms out in opposite directions, his left pointed at Jin. He aimed and fired another bolt of electricity that caused the room to glow with a bluish tint. Yet again, Jin dodged the attack with her fluid reflexes. Jin was almost untouchable when she fought. But even though she wasn't hit, Jin couldn't get close enough to Lucien to land a blow. Lucien surrounded himself with blue electricity, and on top of that, he repeatedly fired off thunderbolts.

So Jin jumped back about ten feet and landed in a low, three-point stance. Her eyes darted left and right. She looked for an opening or something around the room that she could use to his advantage. Before she could even get a look, another shock of electricity erupted near her. This time, she jumped above it and kicked off of the ceiling. This gave her enough of a push to land behind Lucien.

The split moment while he turned to find Jin, she spotted a faucet for a hose a few yards away. In that moment, Lucien sent a torrent of lightning at his opponent. Jin couldn't dodge the blast of energy and was sent flying back several yards into the wall.

Wincing in pain, Jin slumped to the ground. Jin was certain she had broken something, maybe cracked if she was exceptionally lucky. As Lucien moved in to finish her off, Jin kicked off the ground and flipped up so her feet were on the wall. Like a ball, she bounced off the wall and shot away from the blast.

Lucien grunted in frustration. "This is getting old, Jin."

"I would have to agree, old friend."

Lucien laughed, as if that comment was funny. "That's a good one."

As she landed her jump, Jin rolled and then did a cartwheel toward the faucet. Lucien refocused his arms and aimed. He lined up a perfect shot that should have hit Jin. However, she was quicker and more dexterous than anyone Lucien ever fought. The arc of lightning hit the wall near the spigot. The concrete wall ripped like paper from the destructive blast. The crack spread straight down and tore the faucet, causing water to pool around Jin and Lucien.

Lucien, not paying attention to the water starting to pool around him, continued to send volley after volley at Jin. The first cracked the ground beneath Jin as she flipped away from the self-declared lightning meister, and the second was so close it singed her hair. The putrid smell of burnt hair stung her nostrils as Jin flipped off the wall and landed further away from Lucien. He stepped closer to Jin and into the pool of water. Once again, he readied a blast of electricity.

As the lightning surrounded him, a torrent of blue lightning all around him. Then the blue arcs touched the water where he stood, electrifying the water. His body began to spasm and quake from the jolts of electricity that coursed through his body. He dropped to the ground as the lightning died out.

Jin landed and let out a deep sigh. She hadn't had a workout like that in forever. If it wasn't for that stroke of luck, she would have eventually made a mistake. And knowing Lucien, he would have capitalized on it.

***

At that moment, Jake was getting up. He looked a little wobbly, but his face looked no less deterred than before.

Gabriel had to act now. With no practice, and no real idea what he was doing, Gabriel tried to replicate the tele-stasis field.

Like Coach V taught him, he focused on his breathing. He held his hands in front of his chest. His breathing slowed to a calm, regulated tempo. As his breathing slowed, he pushed his hands out toward his sides. He forced all of the telekinetic energy out that he could manage, every ounce of his power.

The area around Gabriel was completely drench in telekinetic energy. With his eyes still closed, he noticed something. He could somehow sense Jake approaching. It was as if, he could see Jake with his telekinesis. His eyes opened, and as he sensed, Jake was right where he had expected.

"What?" Gabriel whispered to himself. "How in the world?"

As Jake moved closer, Gabriel noticed he could sense his movements. Every muscle, he could sense the movement before it happened. He didn't quite understand it, but he could tell what Jake was going to do. But he didn't have time at that moment to contemplate the science of it, because Jake was coming at him.

As Jake moved toward him at a terrible speed, Gabriel could sense Jake was about to plant his foot. His right arm was tensing and closing into a fist. Gabriel could sense his muscles flexing, tightening. Jake was preparing to throw a right haymaker.

Sensing the attack, Gabriel was able to counter. Now, Jake was just a few feet away. Gabriel could sense him now planting that left foot. Gabriel stepped toward Jake, and prepared to throw his own punch. He surrounded the fist with as much telekinetic energy as he could muster after his unorthodox attempt at the tele-stasis field.

Jake's eyes widened, his lips curving into a sneer. Meanwhile, Gabriel stepped into the blow. However, as Jake's fingers clenched and tried to adjust, Gabriel slid around his wildly thrown punch. He stood inches from Jake, and Jake's eyes widened. Gabriel's fist connected with Jake's gut with a surge of telekinetic energy. The force was so potent that Jake lifted off the ground.

Just as Jake landed, Gabriel moved in to finish the fight. Before Jake could react, he wrapped him up in a bear hug to hold his arms down. Immediately, he called to Serena. "Serena, it's now or never!"

Seeing what was going on, Serena picked up on what Gabriel wanted. She focused her mind on Jake and immediately could hear his thoughts. She dove into his subconscious.

***

She was deep inside his mind. Here, inside his subconscious, it was like everything was aflame. His mind was a torrent of anger, of rage, of hatred.

Serena stood there, facing a young man. He seemed gaunt and frail. He was in the fetal position, his hands gripping his knees. He rocked back and forth. At first, she didn't recognize him. But then she realized who this was. In a hurry, she moved to him and knelt beside him. "Jake, are you all right?"

He didn't seem to hear her. His head was tucked into his knees, and his hair was damp with sweat. From above was a voice calling out. It yelled insults.

"You're not strong enough. You're not good enough for the sparring team. You'll never be as strong as them!" It spewed that degrading comment over and over again.

All of a sudden, she realized something as she looked up into the air. It was Jake's own voice that was yelling those things. It was his inner thoughts, his inner insecurities. Then she realized he was whispering. She leaned in to hear what he was saying.

"I'm sorry. I'm sorry. I'm sorry," he was saying over and over again.

"What are you doing here?" said a voice from behind her.

She turned to see Pius. He was standing over them. "'I'm here to take Jake from you. I'm going to break your hold on him."

"Unfortunately, you can't. He's much too far gone for that. You see how fragile he is?" Pius asked.

She looked down at him. *For all his bravado, he's really just as insecure as all of us.* She touched Jake on the shoulder. "Hey, Jake, I want you to listen to me."

He looked up at her as if seeing her for the first time.

"Jake, this isn't your fault. Do you see this man here?" she said pointing at Pius. "He manipulated you. He used your frustration and anger, and he made you turn on your friends. But you can say no."

"How can I stop?" he asked with a quavering voice.

"I want you think about Gabriel, Simon, and all your friends. Can you do that for me?"

Jake nodded meekly.

"Are you thinking about all of us?"

He nodded again with a little more emphasis this time.

"Now focus on that. What feeling comes to you?"

"I don't know. It's like a warmth. I don't really know. Acceptance, I guess."

"Focus on that, Jake. Let that feeling in. Let that feeling overwhelm the anger."

Then all of a sudden, Jake looked up, and he looked like himself again. He looked at Pius, who was baring his teeth at them. "You can't do this!" he said as he rushed at him. But instead of grabbing Jake's arm like he intended, Pius passed right through him.

Serena smiled, "You don't have control anymore, Professor Pius."

***

Back in the real world, Gabriel was holding onto Jake. His body was burning up. It hurt, and Gabriel was screaming from the pain. Then all of a sudden, it stopped. Gabriel let go.

"Did it work?" he asked looking back at Serena. She didn't respond, but her eyes were glowing. "Oh, please in the name of Venus, tell me it worked."

Meanwhile, Jake was grabbing his head as he got to one knee. "What's going on? And why does my head hurt?"

"Well, you see. About that. Uh, so we got into a fist fight?" Gabriel said with a groan, rolling over onto his back.

Meanwhile, Jin was moving in toward Pius. "Pius, by the authority of the Guild and the Protectorate, you are going to be brought in for questioning. As an agent of the Guild, you have the right to remain silent," she said, quoting the lines she had memorized.

Jake was helping Gabriel up, but he was so weak, he immediately had to lean against the pillar before falling. Gabriel caught him before Jake lost his balance.

"Easy buddy. Let's do this together. Support each other," said Gabriel.

They looked at each other. Gabriel noticed the gash under Jake's eye. Likewise, Jake looked at the scar on Gabriel's cheek. "Did I give you that?" asked Jake.

"Yeah," Gabriel answered, "but I gave you one in return." He paused for a second readjusting his leg. "I'm sorry about that."

"Me too," Jake said with a sigh.

"But, hey, at least we have these cool matching scars. It will make us look way cooler from now on."

FILE #23

ANOTHER WHITE ROOM

Jake stood beside a large SUV that was parked half on the lawn beside the Old Cottage. Men and women in suits were running around the lawn around the rundown building. Two agents flanked Jake on both sides. He wasn't quite sure if he was going to be arrested or not.

The woman walked away, but the man was posted there to keep an eye on Jake. Jake made eye contact with the man for a second, and the agent looked at Jake with shifting eyes. His stern face was a mask. Jake didn't blame them for not trusting him. He didn't really trust himself at the moment.

Jake saw Gabriel in an ambulance. They were applying something to his burns. The wounds that Jake must have given him. He didn't remember it, but that's what Gabriel told him. Over by another large vehicle, Serena was putting a blanket around Simon's shoulders. She had gotten him free from Pius's control shortly after the fighting stopped. He felt so thankful for her in that moment. *If she hadn't pulled me back from the edge, I don't know what would have happened to me*, he thought.

Down the way, Coach V was being debriefed by a small team of agents. Gabriel wasn't sure who the girl was. She looked too young to be his boss. But the way she was talking to him, she must have been in charge. Beside her was the man with the white lab coat that they saw when they were fighting Drake last semester.

Then a man with red hair came up to Jake. He wore a buttoned-up vest with a white shirt. He wore no tie unlike most of the other agents. When he stopped in front of Jake, he adjusted his glasses and blew into his hands. He put a cigarette in his mouth and lit it.

"Agent Insomnia. Are you Jake Burns?" he asked with a thick Irish accent.

"Yeah," he answered.

The agent looked at him with a cross expression. "I will be the one taking your statement."

He asked Jake all kinds of questions from the basics to what happened in the basement maybe fifteen minutes ago. He asked Jake about his parents, who Jake told were separated. He asked about siblings, heritage, and more pertinent information like when Jake met Pius. But still, Jake calmly and politely answered each question.

When Jake was asked if his father was *"that* Gideon Burns," he gave an eye roll and said, "Yes, he is *that* Gideon Burns."

***

Afterwards, they were all brought to the Guild base. Well, Jake heard them say it was their current station. Something about their normal base being under investigation. But it didn't really matter. Jake couldn't tell where they were being taken anyways. The windows were tinted so thickly, Jake couldn't see where the base was. The group was brought into a sterile looking waiting room, Jake was pacing. Lucien was sitting at a chair by the door, holding an icepack to his head. Serena was sitting next to him as she was making sure he was clear of any mental control from Pius. She kept asking him how he was or if he needed anything. It was odd seeing this protective side of Serena.

Meanwhile, Simon was lying on the ground with his legs crossed. He was tossing a small ball in the air and catching it. Jin was standing in the corner fixing her hair. But the one person Jake wanted to see wasn't there. Gabriel was in a different room. Hopefully, he was all right.

They had confiscated everyone's phones, so he couldn't check what time it was. Let alone what day it was. Being under Pius's control made Jake's mind really fuzzy. He didn't know much about what had happened the past few days. A few minutes later, an agent came in to speak with Serena. They were discussing the clean-up operation on campus to make sure the other students weren't under Pius's manipulation anymore as well. It sounded like Serena would be helpful in that endeavor.

After waiting for an uncertain amount of time, Agent Insomnia came into the room flanked by two agents. He asked both Lucien and Jin to go with the agent on his right. The agent walked them down a hall. Agent Insomnia then called for Simon and Serena to come with him. The other agent stayed in the room watching over Jake. It was the curly haired young man from before. He leaned against the wall by the door scratching the stubble on his chin. He had an expression of nonchalance, unlike before.

"So, you're Green's friend?" he asked.

"Yeah," Jake answered. "Well, I was. Not sure about that now."

"I guess we're lucky Serena and he handled the situation. Things almost ended up as bad the Drake incident, ya know?" he asked.

"That's for sure."

"I feel a little at fault," he said.

"Why's that?" Jake asked.

"I was supposed to be on campus keeping an eye on Gabriel. But I was called away when Captain Ivy needed support on her trip out."

"Oh, I'm sorry, I guess."

He laughed. "Not your fault, well not really. But, I'm just glad it isn't my burning a…"

Just then, Agent Insomnia came into the room with Coach V. *Or was it Agent V?* Jake wasn't sure.

V came up to him and said, "You want to see them?"

"Yeah, can I?"

Down the hall, they found his room. It was a white hospital room. When they entered, they saw Gabriel sitting on the edge of the bed being examined by the man from before, the man with the white lab coat.

"Is this your friend? The one you were telling me about?" the man in the coat asked Gabriel.

"Yeah, that's him."

"I'll step out and let you two gentlemen talk."

The man and Coach V left, and the two boys were left in silence for several seconds. "I'm kind of worried Jake."

"Oh, yeah. Why's that?" he asked.

"You think I'm going to end up in a hospital room like this every semester?" he said smiling.

"Gosh, you're right. That's two semesters in a row. I hope this is covered under insurance."

"I think it is."

The two laughed. Then Jake came and stood next to him. He saw the wrapped-up burn wounds. "You feeling all right?"

"I'll be fine. They said the burns are bad, but they will heal well. They had a healer on the team come heal them up a bit. But they can't fully do it, ya know?"

"Right."

"How about you?" asked Gabriel.

"I'm okay. My stomach hurts. You must have gotten a good shot in on me, huh?"

"Yeah, sorry about that. I did this weird thing." Gabriel explained how he somehow used his telekinesis to create some kind of radar around himself.

"That's a cool trick."

"Yeah," Gabriel added.

There was a silent pause for a few minutes.

Then Gabriel spoke up. "So, listen man. I've never told anyone this, but when we were fighting, I called you my brother."

Jake looked at him blankly.

"You don't remember that, huh?"

"Na, not at all. I remember when I first started going to the Underground. But then at some point, it just starts to go blank. I guess that's when he got control of me."

"Must be," Gabriel replied. "So, I think of you as my brother. I never had a brother, not really."

"What do you mean, not really?"

"When I was little, my mom was pregnant with a little brother for me. But there was a complication at the hospital. And, well, he didn't make it. For a while my family was so upset, my parents didn't think they wanted kids. But eventually, they had my little sister. She was their miracle baby."

"Wow, man. That's horrible."

Gabriel coughed into his hand. "Yeah, it was. But all of that to say, I think of you as my brother. I will always think about my little brother who I never got to meet, but I still think of you as my brother. Alright."

"Well, we fight like brothers," Jake said, pointing to his scarred eye.

"You're burning right we do," said Gabriel.

A few minutes later, Coach V came into the room. "How are you boys?"

Agent Insomnia came into the room behind him. Coach V shook both of their hands. Agent Insomnia however, stayed in the far corner of the room. "Don't mind me."

V looked both of the boys over. "You two look like you've had a rough night, huh?"

"Sure have," said Gabriel.

"Pretty much," said Jake.

"Well boys. We need to debrief you on the situation a little."

The boys nodded. Coach V put his big hands on their shoulders. Their expressions were that of two kids who were about to get scolded by their parent.

"So, we are working on trying to figure out what part Pius played in this whole thing. But we can assume he was working with Dr. Drake. However, we don't yet know the extent."

"You mean other than trying to make an army of gifted teenagers?" Gabriel asked.

"Well, from what we've been able to piece together from all of the statements is that is not what brought him here. But we think that is why he stayed on campus. Now we need to figure out his end goal."

Gabriel answered, "He said something about taking his army to get back what was his…or something like that."

"So, he is part of something bigger, it would seem," Coach V replied.

"What's going to happen to us?" asked Jake. "Me specifically."

"Well, Jake, you were used and as long as we can prove that what happened was the direct result of Pius, and his misuse of his powers, you shouldn't face any jail time or other consequences. However, the school may make you serve some community service, just to save face."

"I guess that makes sense."

"I'm glad you understand."

"How are you feeling, Gabriel?" Coach V asked.

"I'm all right. A little sore in some places," he said, touching one of his burns. Jake's face fell when he said that.

Coach V picked up on that immediately. "Jake, I want you to listen to me, all right? There is nothing you could have done to prevent this from happening. It isn't your fault."

"But—"

Coach V cut him off. "Nothing you could have done. He took advantage of your emotions, and he manipulated you. His gift allowed him to exploit the frustration you were feeling. Don't let this fester or hurt you. You're best friends. That's all that matters."

Just then, Agent Insomnia stepped in. "Well, I hate to break up this moment, lads. But we have some other things to take care of. This whole situation is impeding on our major mission right now. The investigation of Dr. Drake's lab."

Coach V looked at the boys. "How would you two like to make yourselves useful?"

Epilogue

The sound of a buzz saw filled his ears. Jake put his earbuds in to drown out the sound. The Old Cottage looked different in the day. It was middle of the morning, and he was in charge of cleaning out the remains of the Underground.

The students were told that Professor Pius apparently had some legal troubles and would not be returning, which wasn't too far from the truth.

Jake started stacking all of the chairs on a rolling cart that was designed to hold all of the chairs. As he placed what seemed like the thousandth chair, he looked at the sign across the way. It said, "Welcome to the Underground."

He felt a twinge of guilt. He moved over to the sign and ripped it off the wall. It was made out of solid wood, but he didn't care. His first thought was to set it on fire right there. But instead, he put it on the ground and planted one foot in the center. Then he pulled up on one side of the sign until he heard the loud but satisfying crack.

He put both of the pieces in the center of the concrete floor. There was a snap, and both of the pieces erupted in flames. He sat there, watching the blaze. A flame shone in his eyes. It rose higher and higher. Jake held his hand out as the flames danced around his fingers.

Just then he heard a voice, "That's a waste of good wood."

Jake turned and saw no one. He pulled his headphones off and looked around. *I could have sworn I heard someone...something*, he thought.

He popped the earbuds back into his ears and watched the flames again. He thought about the whole situation. About his friends. He didn't want to do that to them ever again.

"Why do you do that to yourself, Jake?" said the voice from before. He spun around again and scanned the room.

No one. Not a single other soul in the room but him. He walked over to the door and looked down the hallway. Not a sound. He heard the sound of power tools going off upstairs again. The swirling sound of a mechanized drill. The rhythmic sound of a nail gun thumping against beams of wood. But not a single person was down here.

He turned back to face the fire and saw a figure. It was silhouetted by the fire behind him, but it was masculine. His features were all hidden, but the frame was obvious.

"Why are you trying to run from the past, my friend?" said the familiar voice.

"What do you want?" he said.

"I want what I've always wanted. You."

He couldn't be here, Jake thought. He saw them take this man away. He was locked up in a cell and taken far, far away. *So, how in the burning world, was he here*?

"It's quite simple, really," the figure said as if it could hear his thoughts.

"Why's that?" Jake answered.

"This is all in your head," said the figure. He stepped closer to Jake and directly under a hanging light. It lit up his features, and finally Jake could see his face. It was Pius, standing there in his usually well-manicured suit. His hair was pulled back and his small glasses hung on his nose.

"My head?" asked Jake. "What does that mean?"

"Well, you see, I'm not really here. This is just what's left of me. I've apparently drilled so deep into your mind, so deep into your subconscious, that I just live here now. Isn't that wonderful?" Pius asked.

"That sounds like a nightmare," he answered.

"To each his own, I suppose," Pius replied. "But I think I am going to like it here."

About the Author

L. D. Valencia has always loved telling stories. It wasn't until he started his Master's Degree that he was convinced by a student to take his ideas to the published world. He currently lives in the Nashville area with his lovely wife, and he is expecting his first child this year. He hopes to inspire his students to love reading and writing. This book is a testament to that dream. Education is his goal, reading is his passion, and writing is his dream.

Made in the USA
Columbia, SC
15 October 2024

44384988R00105